Cover and Interior book design by One of a Kind Covers

TAINTED CURE
Copyright © by Ashley Fontainne 2016, 2017, 2018

License Notes
This is a work of fiction. Names, characters, places, and incidents are products of the author's imagination or are used fictitiously and are not to be construed as real. Any resemblance to actual events, locations, organizations, or person, living or dead, is entirely coincidental.

This book is licensed for your personal enjoyment only. This book may not be re-sold or given away to other people. If you would like to share this book with another person, please purchase an additional copy for each recipient. If you're reading this book and did not purchase it, or it was not purchased for your use only, then please purchase your own copy. Thank you for respecting the hard work of this author.

Published by RMSW Press, LLC
ISBN-13: 978-0692633106
ISBN-10: 0692633103

TAINTED CURE

SCIENTISTS TRIED TO CURE ADDICTION
THEY FAILED

ASHLEY FONTAINNE

OTHER BOOKS BY ASHLEY FONTAINNE

The Magnolia Series (written with Lillian Hansen):
Blood Ties
Blood Loss
Blood Stain

Mystery/suspense novels:
Fatal Agreements
Suicide Lake
Empty Shell
Night Court
Whispered Pain
Number Seventy-Five

Eviscerating the Snake Trilogy:
Accountable to None
Zero Balance
Adjusting Journal Entries

Paranormal/suspense.
Growl
The Lie
Operation Jade Helmet

Poetry and Short Stories:
Ruined Wings
Fine as Frog Hair
Ramblings of a Mad Southern Woman

TAINTED
CURE

SCIENTISTS TRIED TO CURE ADDICTION
THEY FAILED

ASHLEY FONTAINNE

TABLE OF CONTENTS

Chapter 1 - The Discovery

Two Years Ago - Monday, December 20th – 6:15 a.m.

THE MORNING STARTED OUT LIKE any other inside the cramped space that Everett called home for far too long. His old body rested atop the worn mattress—which was more like a hunk of concrete with an overlay of foam—inside a room no bigger than a small SUV.

Conditioned from years of rising early, he stared at the dark ceiling. He woke up at precisely six-fifteen, just as he'd done since high school. A twinge of stiffness in his back made him groan while exiting the cot. He grabbed what he needed from the small closet, unlocked the gray metal door, and headed to the bathroom.

On autopilot, he showered, dressed, and walked alone down the twisting hallways to the lab, stopping only once on his way to the makeshift cafeteria, and grabbed some black liquid masquerading as coffee for breakfast.

He made it to his destination, leaned down, let the security system scan his retina and waited for the metal door to unlock. Once inside, he donned the white lab coat hanging on the back of his chair, took a swig of tepid coffee, and then made his way over to the rows of cages.

What he saw made the room spin, thus ending the comparison to any other day.

He couldn't seem to remember how to breathe. Blinking proved to be just as difficult. Mouth agape, body rigid, and his butt securely stuck to the uncomfortable chair, a random thought of the time in kindergarten when Jimmy Fassler wiped superglue in Everett's seat popped into his frazzled mind. Hands clammy and sweat pouring from every single gland, his visual cortex struggled to digest the images beaming in from the optic nerves.

Maybe the retina scanner fried my eyes?

It had been ten long, grueling, and life-altering years since his first day at the facility. Eighty-seven thousand, six hundred hours and counting from the moment he'd been blindfolded and ushered inside the ultra-secret laboratory. He still didn't really know where he was, or even if in the United States. He hadn't been out of the compound since his arrival. All he knew was the location was a mile underground. Then again, was that even the truth? That's what he'd been told in clipped, hushed tones while bound, unseen hands of his colleagues— captors, as he referred to them inside his head— leading the way. Because of the sensitive nature of the work and the installation, he could be anywhere.

His stunned mind pulled up memories of the day he'd been hand-picked by the Director of Research, Dr. Roberta Flint. Out of the blue, and reasons still rather uncertain or clear, she recruited him to work on a classified project, code name *Rememdium*.

When Dr. Flint first approached him, he cackled like an onery rooster—hard—once she finished her slick presentation and made the offer. A grim smile tugs at the corners of his mouth while remembering how he'd questioned the woman's sanity and credentials. When he grasped she was serious and the interaction wasn't some sadistic prank, he laughed again. He'd spouted out something rude and uncalled for about the incorrect use of the Latin word for cure as the name of the project. Their conversation roars back…

…"Why in the world should I believe you? The project name isn't even correct! I may be a tad rusty on my Latin, but I seem to recall the word for cure is remedium."

"No, you are correct, Dr. Berning. We simply added our own twist for various reasons we'll discuss later."

"Oh, can't wait. Listen, I can't imagine why you're here and spilling your guts. You said this is a covert operation—the kind only men in black know about—as in off the grid, Area 51 shit."

"Dr. Berning, I assure you only five people outside of the testing facility are aware of Rememdium, including you. Even though you are a civilian, we will grant you the highest level of clearance: Top Secret. We've already performed an SSBI check on you, among others. You passed them all. The next step is for you to accept our terms."

"SSBI check? Others? Non-military terms, please."

"SSBI stands for Single Scope Background Investigation. That's all you need to know for now."

"Yeah, that certainly cleared things up. Exactly what does accepting your terms entail? I'm guessing something along the lines of giving my soul to the good ol' U.S. Government or perhaps burning my fingerprints off and providing me with a code name like E?"

"I appreciate your dark sense of humor, Dr. Berning, however, now is not an appropriate time for jokes. What this means is you will no longer exist, at least as far as the outside world is concerned. Rememdium requires something beyond determination and devotion: personal sacrifice. Discovering the cure will forever alter humanity, although none of us can revel in the glory once we achieve the lofty goal. Our reward will be the immense satisfaction of knowing we helped eradicate addiction. Imagine a world without drug addicts! The ripple effect into other areas of society will be immense and far-reaching—truly game-changing."

"And if I decide not to accept the offer?"

"We already know what skills you possess, Dr. Berning. Your doctoral thesis and late-night blog posts on the subject matter caught our attention. You're just as interested in wiping out addiction as we are—though for a different reason. You won't make the wrong choice."

"I might," Everett countered.

Dr. Flint narrowed her sable brown eyes from the other side of the table inside his miniscule kitchen like he was a meal about to be devoured. Her jet-black hair, beautiful face and dark eyes couldn't hide the icy stare on her face.

Her features hardened like alabaster drying in the scorching desert sun. "We would simply find someone else and assist you in the course you've considered taking many times, doctor. Plain and simple."…

…Pulling himself back to the present, he rubs his eyes. Before the unscheduled—and certainly unexpected—visit by Dr. Flint, Everett had been a broken man. He'd lost his job as Director of Research Administration Services at Emory University after turning to alcohol to numb the pain from the accident that destroyed his world. He worried he would never get past the overwhelming loss of his entire family if he didn't move, so he left Atlanta and returned to Little Rock, Arkansas, soon after the deaths of his wife, children, parents, and in-laws. Sorrow overshadowed every thought, threatening to drown him in the storm of grief.

His previous life ended in seconds when a driver high on methamphetamine with a blood alcohol level over 2.0, t-boned the SUV driven by his father-in-law, Bertrand. The family outing for an afternoon of shopping and bowling was over in mere seconds inside a pile of charred metal on Peachtree Avenue.

One week before Christmas.

A trip he begged off from because he had reports to finish before the holiday break.

After moving into the old house left to him by his grandparents, he filled the lonely days teaching chemistry and microbiology to students at a local technical college, which was the only job he could find after falling from academic grace. The students were more interested in posting, tweeting, sharing, and tagging shit on the Internet than learning about science. Though frustrating, he pushed the annoying traits of the next generation out of his daily thoughts.

With the entire group of his loved ones no longer a part of his life, he contemplated killing himself four separate times, each in different ways—how Dr. Flint knew that he was still a mystery. Every time he came close, something inside his mind whispered to wait. Forced his hand to remove the gun from his mouth; stopped the same hand millimeters from quivering lips before depositing a handful of sleeping pills. The hesitant voice in his mind made him pause before putting the garden hose in the exhaust pipe of his vehicle, and step on the brake pedal before going over a cliff.

The clinical side of his brain considered killing healthy tissue a waste. The emotional side craved for the last-minute changes of heart to be from his deceased wife, Carol, reaching across the dimensions to stop him.

His hatred for drugs started the day his life imploded.

Taking up Dr. Flint's edict to find a cure for addiction did not require much persuading on her end. Even the not-so-veiled threat about killing him if he decided not to take the job wasn't what swayed his decision.

Finding a cure—permanently, so no one else would suffer like he had—was the catalyst. He'd convinced his shattered mind that's why he was still alive, the reason he was a scientist, and why Dr.

Flint selected him to lead the charge in discovering an end to the worldwide scourge of addiction.

He shakes the old memories away as his wits return. The time for ruminating in the past is over. It is time to revel in the victories of the present and soak up the elusive moment ten years in the making.

A twinge of sadness makes his chest clench when glancing at the calendar on the wall: December 20th. Exactly eleven years since his old life ended. Out of habit, his thumb finds the wedding band still on his ring finger, rubbing the smooth platinum.

Sorry it took me so long. I love you all and miss each of you every day. Hope you are watching this. I'm on the cusp of making history!

Limbs working once more, he snatches the report sheet from the desk he'd set there twelve hours prior. Age-spotted fingers tremble while reading the notes on formula number 10,899, administered the night before to the test subject labeled the same.

It worked.

The little white mouse sits quietly at the opposite end of its enclosure. Born from a long lineage of addicted rodents, bred to study the physical and genetic qualities of addicts, the change is downright astonishing. It is uninterested in the heroin sitting in the food dish less than ten inches away. Instead, the mouse busies itself by cleaning its whiskers.

He had dubbed the specimen *Ultima Mus*—the last mouse—because if the latest chemical compound failed, he planned on giving up. The long days, sleepless nights, and haunted dreams drained the last ounce of strength to continue. He already had his exit plan from the world mapped out.

He finds his voice and shouts, "Riverside! Come here!"

From across the lab, fellow researcher Dr. Daryl Riverside flinches. Everett rarely speaks and when he does, his normal tone and cadence are quiet and unassuming.

He tries, but cannot recall, the last time he'd spoken the kid's name. Two months? Three?

Riverside jumps to his feet, long legs making short order of the distance between them. His tennis shoes make strange noises on the vulcanized rubber floor while walking toward Everett.

Daryl's unruly dark curls bounce in harmony with his steps. "What's wrong, Dr. Berning? Did you cut your hand again?"

Everett laughs at the young pup's concern for his older lab partner. "No, though I would have cut off an appendage for these results."

Daryl slides to a stop, his light, hazel eyes wide with shock and curiosity while staring at Ultima. He pushes the hair from his face and peers closer. "Are you saying—?"

Everett grins. The moment is the first time he's felt happy—truly happy—in over ten years.

Grabbing Riverside by the neck, he hugs the bewildered kid tight. "Yes! We did it! Look at that! Ultima has no interest in the heroin! Of course, we still need to run a battery of tests on him—see what, if any, side effects the formula might have on his organs. Oh, and we also need to run tests on the additional subjects hooked on various other drugs."

Releasing Riverside from the hug, he paces in front of the cages, mind racing with a thousand thoughts while putting together a mental laundry list of the next procedures.

Daryl laughs and pats Everett's shoulder. "Calm down, Doc. Wouldn't want to have a stroke or heart attack, right? What fun would it be to die before you were one-hundred percent sure?"

Everett ignores the stupid comment, excitement coursing through him. He feels twenty years younger as he moves to the counter and scribbles notes. "Where's Dr. Flint?"

***

Robert Flint takes a long gulp of iced green tea to clear the fog inside her mind. Being so far underground interferes with her circadian rhythm. Over the years, the group of nerve cells inside her brain controlling her master clock finally calmed down, allowing some semblance of normal sleep.

Then menopause took control of her body four months ago. The onset screwed up her insides even worse than the subterranean hellhole she'd called home for over ten years. If she suffered one more bout of night sweats and hot flashes, her plan was to sleep naked on rubber sheets with a bag of ice on her head. She couldn't begin to imagine how rough the annoying symptoms would be if she were above ground. The heat and humidity would cause her to spontaneously combust. For the first time in years, she was glad she was underground.

Though a scientist, she refuses to ingest man-made chemicals to ease the symptoms. The change is part of the normal progression of aging. Since she never wanted—nor had—children, there was no pangs of melancholy like most other females. She embraced what her mother called "the last leg of a woman's race" with gusto.

Since she had zero desire to become a mother, there were no psychologically induced alarm bells ringing inside her head, warning her the expiration date of her eggs neared. Her lips curl in disgust at the thought of giving birth, spending every waking moment consumed with taking care of a helpless thing completely dependent upon its mother for survival. Not to mention the damage to a woman's body as the cluster of cells grew. No man, no matter how well-endowed or loving, was worth a lifetime of servitude to some ungrateful brat. Besides, she would never let the twelve years she'd spent in med school go to waste.

Personally, she didn't miss the cramps and torrent of blood each month, though she did miss the week or so of mood swings. Her entire career had been spent working alongside males, and all of them seemed pre-programmed to assume all women suffered from PMS. She never had major shifts in mood during her cycle, though she never let anyone else in on her little secret. The false assumption she would get "bitchy" each month gave her a chance to let out some anger every three weeks if anyone got too close.

She did miss that.

Roberta would have to simply ride out the symptoms for the next few months until her body acclimated to the shift in hormone levels. She just needed to ignore the irritating side effects until the readjustment was complete. Hormone replacement therapy is an option, yet she staunchly refused to chemically alter what nature intended.

She let out a snort of derision at the thought.

What a hypocrite I am!

Once situated in front of the computer screen, she sighs. Temperature regulated, she shrugs off the previous thoughts and concentrates on the tasks at hand, giving a quick scan of the small office. No expense had been spared in creating the research headquarters. Though it had no windows the rest of the interior is flawless. The slick construction and attention to detail hid the fact they were underground.

Technological advances were grand in terms of medical research. The equipment throughout the entire facility is a joy to work with—when she had the opportunity—and worth well over ten million dollars. Using the expensive gadgets excites her yet reading and typing out emails frustrates her beyond words.

Today, she has twenty-seven unopened emails vying for attention. Several of the messages are from Dr. Jason Thomas, her immediate superior and occasional romp-in-the-sack partner when he made impromptu appearances. A small grin turns her full lips upward. Seeing his name reminds her over six weeks have passed since their last dalliance. A twinge of sexual heat warms her groin.

At least her hormone levels are still high enough that she hasn't lost interest in sex.

She clicks on the most recent email, one requesting a daily status update, glances at her watch, and grimaces. "My, but aren't we impatient this morning? Perhaps I am not the only one suffering with hormonal balance issues."

After a cursory glance through the other emails, she scowls. No status report from Dr. Berning. How odd. The phone rings so she reaches across the desk to answer. Tardiness is something she expects from Dr. Riverside, not the always punctual Everett.

The LED indicates the call is from Dr. Berning's station. "Good timing, Dr. Berning. I was just about to—"

"Sorry, but today's report requires you see with your eyes first. At this moment, I'm not sure I could stop my fingers from shaking long enough to type out a legible word."

"Expound, please." She furrows her brow, unaccustomed to hearing any emotion other than boredom or a twinge of sadness from Dr. Berning.

"Roberta, just get down here. I'm serious!"

"Did you just refer to me as—?"

"No time for formalities. I'm too excited. We did it. We fucking did it!"

Before she can respond, the call disconnects. The excitement in Dr. Berning's voice makes her own heart rate spike. She stares at the email from Jason and considers shooting him a reply yet decides against it.

He'll just have to wait a while longer. If what Everett said is true, Jason won't bat an eye at her late response.

In a flash, she rises from the chair and bounds down the hallway toward the main lab.

It has to be true—no one at the facility ever used her first name.

Ever.

Chapter 2 - Another Day at the Office

Monday, December 20

Monday, December 20th – 10:00 p.m.

BENITO SAN NICOLAS ADMIRES THE opulent décor of the bedroom, gaze taking in the party decorations for his birthday. It is the first time he's noticed how stunning the place is since he usually blocks out all the other times he's been inside the room.

He smiles, exposing a set of perfectly white, capped teeth, settling his focus on the monster strapped to the chair in the middle of the floor. The dark brown eyes of his captured prey stare back with a mixture of fear and defiance. For a few seconds, he drinks in the intoxicating view of Mario's fat body bound to the seat. The anticipation of the kill makes Benito's pulse pound. The rush is better than any drug or sex act.

Removing his jacket, Benito rolls up his sleeves, eager to usher in his reign. His gaze never wavers from the soon-to-be former *Capo*. The only sounds in the room are his own footsteps reverberating off the marble floors and Mario's labored breathing. His devilish grin widens while walking over to the tray of weapons next to Mario.

His fingers hover over the tools as if contemplating which one to use though he's already chosen inside his mind. Beads of sweat form on

Mario's haggard, old skin, right next to droplets of blood from where Benito hit him earlier. A few trickles of both drip off a bulbous nose and onto the stained, once white t-shirt.

"So, *chero*, here we are. What a way to celebrate my twentieth birthday, eh? I'm sure the reversal of our roles wasn't something you'd expected. *Esta bien yucca, no?*"

Mario Alvarado's jaw tightens, and he swallows hard. "You knock me out, tie me up like some common *Halcones*—in my own *casa*—and still address me as friend? Pft! You are wrong. The situation isn't difficult for you. Only me."

"I disagree, Mario. I'm seconds away from creating a masterpiece out of your body, yet no one will ever know the handiwork is mine. I find that incredibly difficult and rather sad. Ah, the life of an artist is filled with disappointments, no?"

Benito licks his lips while clasping damp fingers around the brand new Bushlore knife. Gripping the Micarta handle, he raises his arm high, admiring the glint off the overhead lights on the blade.

"When I found you, you were nothing but a *chucho*, begging for food and shelter in the filth-stained back alleys in San Salvador!" Mario yells, sending flecks of white spittle from his mouth, which stick to his dark mustache. "This is how you repay me? *Puchica!*"

His movements are lightning fast. Before Mario utters another sound, Benito pushes the tip of the sharp blade against the tub of lard's throat. A thin sliver of red appears and dribbles down the metal.

"Do you think I'm not grateful you rescued me, Mario? Made me a *Lugarteniente*? You provided me with an education, training, and a deep understanding of the business world. I'm thankful you bestowed upon me the title of Lieutenant over hundreds of men. Had you not whisked me away, I'd still be, as you say, a dog in the streets, perhaps even already dead. While I appreciate those things, the price you made me pay—nightly—for the rescue was harsh. Very harsh. Your bedroom tutoring turned this mongrel into a ravenous wolf, one who is now ready to lead the pack. Enough idle chit-chat. Let's get down to business. Tell me the combination to the safe. I want whatever secret you are hiding inside. I already know everything else necessary to take your place."

Mario's foul, hot breath grazes Benito's cheek. The sensation brings back disturbing memories of the nights of pain and torture endured at the hands of his mentor when younger. Seething rage pumps through his body, begging to be unleashed.

Benito forces his eager hands to wait.

In a last-ditch effort to control the situation, Mario whispers, "You may ascend to the top now, but one day, you'll be the old dog. The pack is full of scheming members just waiting for the time to strike. They may bow to your whims now, drooling over whatever reward you dangled in front of them to betray me. Yet one day, just as you've done to, they'll turn and sink their teeth into you. Do your best. I am not afraid. I won't tell you a damned thing. My secrets are mine alone."

Benito traces a slow line with the tip of the blade from Mario's neck, stopping directly above his belt line. With a flick of his wrist he cuts through the material, exposing the flaccid instrument Mario tormented him with for years.

"You've never been more wrong, *chero*. What is yours is now mine. All of it."

Minutes later, the room still ringing with the delightful screams of his former boss and his own demented laughter after Mario yelled out the combination, Benito ascended the throne as the next *Capo* of El Salvador's largest drug cartel.

Turning to stare at the bloody, unrecognizable pile of flesh in the chair, Benito whispers, "Happy birthday to me."

***

Though nearly midnight, the unseasonable heat and humidity cling to the night air with a ferocious grip. With only one week until Christmas, the temperature feels like mid-September, and Regina Parker groans. Enduring one summer per year in Arkansas is enough. The second she turns off the motor, familiar wetness pools underneath her arms and vest.

Only three other vehicles are in the parking lot of the small building serving as the PD. The black Dodge Charger is hers, and the tan Ford Minivan belongs to the city of Rockport's only radio dispatcher, Eugenia "Geenie" Renfro. An old Chevy truck held together by rust and a Southern favorite—duct tape—sits directly in front of the station. At one time, the ancient thing had been red and silver, but time removed the original color, and only those who'd lived in the town for more than ten years could remember what it looked like before.

She chuckles to herself, wondering how much longer the old hunk of metal has before leaving its owner, Officer Roger Singleton, stranded on the side of the road.

Once inside the station, she hears Geenie whining about the warm temperature in the front office. "I swear I'm just gonna turn into a big ol' pile of damp clothes. A nice, cool winter is supposed to be our reward for tolerating hotter-than-Hades summers!"

"My grandma surely agrees with you on that count, Ms. Eugenia." Roger laughs. "If I was a betting man, I'd lay money down she's eaten two whole boxes of popsicles in the last three days."

Regina walks up to the duo and joins the conversation, forcing herself not to stare at Roger's awful haircut. The dark auburn locks look like he stuck his head underneath a weed whacker. She pictures Roger's eighty-year-old grandmother snipping away his curls at the kitchen table in the house they share. "Weather report on the radio earlier said temps should return to normal by Wednesday. They said there's a thirty percent chance of snow on Christmas Eve."

Geenie crinkles her nose and laughs. A damp lock of over-processed blonde hair flops onto her chubby cheek. "This is Arkansas. Weather can change in the blink of an eye. Evening, Chief."

Roger adjusts his hat before wiping a trickle of sweat from his wide brow. He tips the worn-out Stetson. "Evening, boss lady. How was it tonight?"

Regina reaches past the youngest of Rockport's two other law enforcement figures and hands her ticket book to Geenie. At only twenty-four, Roger Singleton is young enough to be her son. A hint of his cologne invades the space between them, making her nose twitch. The stuff reeks.

"Fairly quiet until around eight. That's when Kirk Sorrells decided to test out his latest batch of moonshine. I'm never going to get the image of his flabby, naked ass running down Highway 270. Ever. Corralling him into my unit might require extensive therapy to forget. I'm giving serious consideration to adding a plastic cover over the backseat."

"Is he in the hole?" Roger grins and motions toward the single holding cell at the back of the building.

"Yep. Sleeping it off. I didn't feel like taking him all the way to the county jail. Figured the less time he spent naked in my backseat, the better. I cited him for public indecency. When he wakes up, he can go home. At least when he goes before Judge Harmon, he'll have clothes on. Ha, the poor judge will probably have to work at keeping a straight face after reading my report."

"You didn't give him a public intox charge?"

"Roger, giving the old fart another expensive charge isn't going to make him stop drinking." Regina exits the door, fumbling around for the car keys in her front pocket. "Only rehab will. I plan on talking to Judge Harmon about that tomorrow morning. The man's already living hand-to-mouth. Taking more money from Kirk's pocket will just drive him to work harder on his side business, and drink even more."

Roger's gaze settles on the hood of his truck, a sad smile crossing a set of thin lips. "That ain't like you, Chief. Your change of heart wouldn't have anything to do with Jesse's troubles, would it?"

She bristles at the mention of her daughter.

Most of the time, she enjoys living and working in a small town with a population of less than a thousand, except for moments like now. The many perks of the quaint town kept her from moving to a bigger city, along with strong family ties to the rural area. She was the fifth generation born and raised in the tiny berg and the first female and second family member to hold the title of Chief of Police.

Everybody looks out for each other. The community is tight knit. Unfortunately, the flip side is everyone's business is everyone's business. The gossip train travels at break-neck speeds. Within an hour after taking a strung-out Jesse to Bright Waters Treatment Center in North Little Rock two weeks ago, all of Rockport knew. Proof of their knowledge arrived when her cell phone blew up with calls from dozens of concerned citizens offering their condolences and support. Several of the ladies from First Park Baptist brought over enough casseroles and salads to last her two full weeks. They even held hands and prayed for God to take away Jesse's cravings for meth.

"Maybe." Shaking off the horrible memory, Regina steps up her pace and reaches her car. "I've learned quite a bit about how addiction works lately in counseling. One of the top spots on the list is financial stressors. Addicts don't handle life's little ups and downs very well. Money trouble is sometimes a trigger. Kirk needs rehab, not jail time or additional bills to pay. He's been outta work for three years ever since the sawmill closed."

Roger cocks his head, a look of shock across his face. "Huh. I'll be. Never thought I'd hear those words leave your mouth. If anyone asks me about your change of heart, I'll tell them it's from this God-awful heat. Wouldn't want our citizens to think their hard-nosed chief of police is getting all sentimental in her old age."

Ignoring the jab, she slides behind the wheel of the Charger. She grins at the rumble of the 5.7-liter engine. She can tell Roger is still talking yet she chooses to pretend she doesn't notice, gives the car some gas, and lets the parking lot fill with the Charger's deep growls from the dual exhaust.

Without saying another word, she leaves and heads home. A lump of sadness sticks in the pit of her stomach knowing the house will be empty, making her want to hit something to release the churning anger inside her mind.

She won't let the tears come. She shed enough the day she left Jesse in rehab. Other than Fred's funeral and the death of her parents, she had never cried so hard. The salty mess clouded her vision while she trudged—alone—back to the car. Jesse had bounced between rage-fueled screams of hatred to tear-filled pleas for her not to leave. The look of terror and fear on Jesse's face when Regina walked out the door made her chest clench with sorrow. By the time she made it, the wracking sobs were so intense she couldn't do a thing except lean against the doorframe and squall like a lost kitten.

"Not gonna do it! No crying today!" Regina cranks up the radio as "Catch Scratch Fever" blares throughout the interior. At the top of her voice, she belts out the words alongside Ted Nugent, grateful for the distraction.

Five minutes later, she pulls into the driveway of the small, three-bedroom house she shares with Jesse. Turning off the car, she stares at the place. Visions of the day the ownership papers were signed replay inside her mind. A week before their first anniversary, alongside her husband Fred, they'd moved in. Less than a year later, Jesse was born.

Memories of Jesse running around in excitement while she watched them decorate the roofline with colored lights makes her chest ache. Without the usual over-the-top light display, the house looks dreary and sad, matching her mood to perfection.

"Christmas is gonna suck this year," she mutters while biting her lip. A straggler tear escapes and tumbles down her cheek. "I miss you, Fred. So much. Maybe you could have kept Jesse from using drugs. I sure failed. Damnit! This wasn't how we'd planned things. I need you here. Doing all this alone is gonna break me right in two."

Her cell phone buzzes with an incoming call. Exiting the car, she grins. Ever since they were born, the bond between her and Reed is sometimes eerie. "Your timing is perfect as usual. I was on the verge of a major pity party."

"One of the many perks of being a twin is sensing disturbances in our mutual force." Reed's laughter is deep and melodic. "So, you home now? How was your shift?"

Unlocking the front door, she flicks on the lights and holds in a deep sigh. Though she loves Reed with ferocity, hearing his voice makes her miss his presence even more. He'd moved to Laredo, Texas over twenty-five years ago after joining U.S. Customs and Border Patrol. When Fred was still alive, they made the yearly trek to Laredo for Christmas. The tradition ended when Fred died. After Jesse ran away, Regina refused to go, choosing not to celebrate the holidays without her daughter. The plan to revive the holiday visit on her own ended when she found Jesse two weeks ago. She hadn't seen her brother since Fred's funeral, and she misses him more than she is willing to admit out loud.

"I'm sure not quite as exciting as yours. Aren't you supposed to be keeping our borders safe from drugs and bad guys?"

"Only on days I'm at work."

Stopping in mid-stride, goosebumps appeared on her arms and neck. "You aren't in Laredo, are you? Don't tell me you drove over seven-hundred miles...?"

Racing to the front room, she pushes the curtains aside and peeks out the window. Headlights blink twice then shut off. Under her breath she mutters, "I'll be damned!"

Tossing her phone onto the couch, she opens the door and steps outside. Reed climbs out from behind the wheel of his SUV and in seconds, his hulking 6'4" frame lumbers up the driveway to the porch. He flings his beefy arms around her shoulders.

"You should have told me you were coming! You know, given me a chance to cook or..."

"Which is exactly why I didn't give you fair warning." Reed steps back, smiles, and holds up a sack of food with a big, red bow on top. The smells wafting from inside give away the fact it is Italian. "You can't cook for squat. Here, take this inside so I can get my bags."

"Ass." She gives Reed's arm a playful smack. "Wait, bags? And what's the deal with the freaking bow? Your way of saying Italian take-out is what you got me for Christmas?"

"Yes, bags. They come in quite handy when someone moves. You know, to store all your belongings in? Ain't no way I'd let the movers handle my treasured collection of hats and boots."

Her heart thuds inside her chest as she looks down at the bag and notices a note is attached. Reaching inside the door, she flips on the porch light and peers at the paper. Written in her brother's atrocious scrawl, it reads, "An Italian feast to celebrate my retirement."

"You…retired? Boots? Hats? Are you moving back for good?" She stops as her voice cracks with emotion while watching her brother amble up the steps carrying two large suitcases.

"Yep. I need to be here to help my niece. Oh, and you. You're sort of a scatterbrain at times. Then again, the bowl of lemons you've been handed hasn't helped much. The way I figured, you needed someone rough and tough to lean on. Remember all the years you've given me grief about not marrying or having kids and I always said I had my reasons? Well, taking care of you and yours would be one of them."

Reed grins and walks past her, turning his body sideways while passing through the threshold. Dumbstruck, she stares at his rigid back, overwhelmed with emotions.

He's home. Thank God.

Rather than bursting into tears from the amazing turn of events, she shuts the door and follows him inside.

Just as she's done her entire life, she resorts to humor in an emotional situation. "Glad you're here, bro, but if you start snoring, you're sleeping on the porch."

Reed sets the bags in the middle of the floor and grins. "Fair enough. Same goes for you. Now, enough chatting. Time to eat. I've been on the road a long time and I'm starved."

Shaking her head at the crazy turn of events, she heads into the kitchen to fix their plates, deciding Christmas won't be so bad after all, and says a silent thank you to Fred for convincing the powers above to give her some support.

***

Jason Thomas fumbles with the zipper on the sports bag. He doesn't have the time or patience to dick around with a temperamental piece of cheap metal. Though never a patient person by design, his allotted quota seemed to diminish at the same rate his hair started to disappear. At the current rate of hair loss, by the time he turns sixty-eight the well of patience will be empty.

Grinding his teeth to keep from screaming, he tries one last time, finding success. Nerves on edge from the last fifteen hours, he yanks the bag from the bed. The day had passed by in a blur of activity and he is ready for the quiet drive to the facility. The phone call from Roberta—the one he'd waited on for over a decade—sent his mind and body into high gear.

"You about ready, Dr. Thomas?"

Jason shakes his head at the familiar voice from the doorway. "Almost, Dirk. Just finished packing. I need to shut down my laptop and then I'll be on my way."

Dirk Kincanon steps inside, reaching down to pick up the bags. "Which vehicle are you taking?"

The tone in Dirk's voice would have irked him any other time, but considering what is at stake, and how excited he is about Dr. Berning's discovery, he opts to let the infraction slide. The heated discussion between the two of them several hours ago about his decision to drive—alone with no security detail through the Ozark Mountains— ended on a sour note. Dirk, his trusted confidant, and right-hand man, still appears miffed about the exchange.

"Black Ram. Rednecks won't bat an eye at yet another Bubba truck tooling around in the hills."

Dirk gives a faint nod of approval. "First good choice you've made today, sir."

"Dirk—enough. I appreciate your concern for my well-being. Really. Protecting me is one of the reasons I hired you, however, you know why I need to go alone and why I won't budge on my stance. Now, quit worrying. This is a time for celebrating. I won't tolerate another dig. Do I make myself clear?"

"Crystal, sir."

He watches the hulk of a man heft the bags and exit the bedroom. Dirk's body language conveys his irritation and concern just as well as his words from seconds ago. Rather than dwelling on Dirk's annoyance, he walks over to the desk and shuts down the laptop, secures it inside the titanium case, and then glances at his watch. It is almost ten p.m., which will put him at the facility in less than two hours, barring any traffic. The decision to wait to leave, timing his arrival just right, was made to keep up the appearance he'd traveled much further than the actual distance. Though the truth about the entire operation will eventually be revealed if this is truly the news he's been yearning to hear, he knows the time isn't right just yet.

Briefcase in hand, he makes his way across the expanse of the large bedroom, stopping to pick up one last item to accompany him on the journey.

The eight-by-ten color photo sits inside a gold-rimmed frame. The smiling faces of his young wife, Laresa, and their twin girls, Tasha and Tanya, stare back in silence. A moment frozen on film from the flash of a camera, taken on the front lawn of the grand estate the Thomas family called home. The picture had taken over fifteen shots to perfect because their St. Bernard, Benny, wouldn't hold still. Tasha and Tanya kept erupting into a pile of giggles as Benny bounded in between them.

Picking it up to look closer, he swallows the lump of tears trapped inside his throat. Tasha and Tanya were almost ten and mirror images of their beautiful mother. Each sported thick, honey-blonde hair and eyes so blue strangers asked if they were wearing contacts. The girls were already tall and lanky for their ages, and both possessed their mother's grace and agility. He often joked that his children were clones of their mother and his only contribution to their genetic makeup was their proclivity for the sciences.

Unwilling to continue down memory lane, he opens the briefcase and slides the photo inside. He rarely leaves the estate but when he does venture out, he never leaves without the picture of his reasons for living. Laresa, Tanya, and Tasha are the guiding forces behind his quest to end addiction. Every penny, every single moment, all done in memoriam of the three most important people in his life.

With one final glance around the room, he is satisfied he's packed all items necessary for the trip, so he shuts the door and punches in the security code, thus sealing the area off from others while he is away.

Dirk is waiting for him at the bottom of the staircase, his normally pale face dotted with splotches of red.

"The truck's running and I topped off the tanks. Already punched in the coordinates to the lab. There's a full first aid kit and plenty of supplies..."

Jason holds up his hand. "I'm quite confident you've prepared the vehicle way beyond the point of necessity, Dirk. Should I encounter engine trouble, or worse, I'm sure there's enough stored inside to keep me alive for days. I'll contact you via text upon my arrival. Remember—not a word to the others I've departed. Maintain status quo. Until I am one hundred percent satisfied this is truly the moment we've been working toward, I don't want any false hope to pervade the others."

Dirk sighs as he follows Jason out to the garage. "As you wish, Dr. Thomas."

Once inside the garage, Jason opened the truck door and secures the briefcase in the passenger seat. After climbing behind the wheel, he looks at Dirk's concerned face. He can tell the man is fighting the urge to say something else.

"Something else on your mind, Dirk?"

"Actually, yes. Have you considered how those at the lab will react when you show up alone? And in civilian clothes? None of them have ever seen you without an entourage. Don't you think they'll be suspicious?"

He laughs. "Dirk, what little faith you have in me. I have a freshly pressed uniform inside my bag and will change into it prior to my arrival. With all the excitement going on at the lab, I doubt anyone will notice I'm alone. If they do and ask me about it, I'll simply tell them my escorts are above-ground, guarding the location from any would-be intruders because we don't want word to get out about the discovery. That will satisfy their curiosity. After all, they are just as worried about security as we are. Mind the estate for me, Dirk. I'll let you know if we have truly been successful or not."

Dirk's gaze is harsh and full of doubt. "You really think they have, Dr. Thomas? I mean, they've been close before, only to realize they were wrong."

He touches his belly while grimacing at the slight paunch he'd recently developed. "My gut tells me this isn't a drill. It's the real deal. Better be. My old ticker might not be able to handle another bout of disappointment. Please open the door. It's time for me to hit the road."

Without another word, Dirk moves away from the cab and over to the side of the garage. The metal door groans as it opens, revealing the pitch-black forest surrounding the mansion. Jason rolls the window up, turns on the air conditioner, and smiles while making his way down the long drive.

Chapter 3 - Prepping

Wednesday, December 22nd – 9:00 p.m.

WALTER "WALT" ADDISON STOPS and motions behind him for Turner to do the same. The crunch of their footfalls on the bed of dry leaves is barely audible, drowned out by the nocturnal rumblings of insects in the forest.

"What's wrong, Dad? Why are we stopping?" Turner whispers.

"Getting my bearings straight, that's all. Now be quiet before you give our position away."

"Ain't nothing out here but us—"

"Hush, Turner!"

Walt's sharp gaze scans the tree line as Turner remains silent. Once dark, he and Turner left deer camp and headed deep into the woods. They'd been trekking through the Ozark Forest, their path illuminated by the full moon and aided by the warm weather, for nearly an hour. When they made the same journey last hunting season, the temperature wasn't even in the double digits. The weird, warm weather isn't any good for hunting, yet it made the trip easier.

An uneasy feeling settles over him while peering into the woods. He knows the area better than his own backyard. Walt remembers exactly where every tree, boulder, path, and cliff is located leading up to the cave.

After a stint in the Army, Walt came to the realization the world was too screwed up to continue. Seeing up close and personal what Uncle Sam was capable of, along with the corrupt governments of other countries, left him a bitter and paranoid man. When Curt Campbell, a coworker, and an ex-Army man, invited Walt to a meeting one night after work, he jumped at the chance. Curt mentioned the small group was full of other men who were dedicated to keeping their families safe during troubling times.

The initial meeting had been over twenty years ago, and it solidified his decision to prepare himself and his family for the end of civilized society. Though most of his stockpiles of supplies were at home, he figured a back-up plan was needed as well. While hunting alone twelve years prior, he'd stumbled upon the cave quite by accident. Even though it was located on government land, he didn't care. The place wasn't listed or notated on any map he'd surveyed over the years.

"Dad, are we close? My arms are getting tired."

He turns and stares at his only child. Though Turner is twenty and just as tall and lithe as Walt, sometimes the boy acts like a bratty teenager. "What part about hush don't you get, son?"

"Won't do any good to keep lugging these supplies if they're all busted. These canning jars are heavy!"

"Fine," Walt huffs. "Set it down. You need to increase your training. More cardio and weights are what you need. When things get to crunch time—"

"I need to be ready. Yes, Dad. I know." Turner interrupts while easing the heavy pack onto the ground. "Cut me some slack, will you? It takes a while to fully recover from the flu."

"It's been three days, Turner. You're fine." Walt mumbles while scanning the perimeter. Seeing nothing, but unable to shake the strange sensation something is wrong, he walks over to join his son.

"Want to tell me what's really going on? We've been making this hike ever since I was little. Bearings my ass."

Squatting down, Walt peers at the trail. The hairs on his neck and arms stand erect when noticing footprints. With a nod of his head, he points them out to Turner. "See those? They're fresh, maybe a day or so old. Note the tread. Those are government issued boots. I knew it! Someone's been out tromping around here. You best start learning to rely on your instincts, son, or you ain't never gonna survive when the world turns to shit."

Turner swallows and leans forward, squinting in the dark. "How in the world did you notice those, Dad?"

Motioning for his son to get up and follow, Walt whispers, "Because I pay attention to my gut. I knew the minute we came over the ridge something wasn't right. Come on, we need to follow these prints and see if they lead to the cave. Not another word until we know for sure. I mean it. Zip your hole."

Turner groans and picks up the pack and follows him down the path.

Minutes later, Walt stops and lets out a heavy sigh. "Whoever was out here didn't find the cave. See? The prints lead the other direction. They veered off and headed west. Just to be safe, give me the pack. Stand guard while I go add to our supplies and check things out. Do not move from this spot until I call for you. Got it?"

"Dad, you sure? What if someone's inside?"

"Don't worry about your old man, boy. I'll introduce them to this." He pulls back the jacket to reveal the nine-millimeter nestled inside his waistband. "Now, sit tight until I return. Keep your mouth shut and eyes peeled for trouble. If you spot any, don't hesitate to use force. This here cave belongs to the Addison clan and no one else."

Turner nods and hands over the pack. Walt situates the bag on his shoulders before taking off at a light trot, heading for the hidden entrance to the cave.

***

Turner Addison licks his dry lips over and over, trying to calm his overtaxed nerves. All the repetitive movement does is make the cracks in his skin worse. The bark of the tree he leans against pokes through the thin jacket, making his skin itch. The cicadas are louder than before and the noise level raises his edginess. How is he supposed to hear a two or four-legged predator nearby over the ruckus?

"Get a grip. Dad will flip out if he finds me a bundle of sweat and all jittery. I'll never hear the end of it. Then the entire trip back to camp, I'll be forced to endure stories of his time in the military."

Chuckling to himself, he scanned the area. With all the leaves gone except for a few pine trees interspersed throughout the groves of others, he has a clear view of the surroundings. The silver light of the moon gives the entire area a spooky feel. A shiver of fear ambles up his back when he thinks about all the horror movies he's watched over the years. Lone people in the woods end up as victims of some crazed, knife-wielding psycho.

He hates skulking around in the woods and despises the fact his father is a prepper just as much. Hunting isn't so bad, only because his dad closes the machine shop every year during muzzleloader, bow, and gun season. Turner enjoys the time away from work though he wishes he could spend the free time pursuing things that interested him, not his father. Stalking animals and then having to gut and haul away the meat turns his stomach. He really wants to hang out with friends and play video games, but those things are not on the list of approved activities by his overbearing father.

He's considered moving out of his childhood home several times, yet each time he gets close, ends up staying. With only a high school education and limited job skills of working at the machine shop, financially, he is stuck under the eaves of 145 Windsong Lane, at least for the foreseeable future. Living life alone is expensive. He'd researched all available rental houses and trailers in Hot Spring County, but without a roommate, would never be able to swing the bills on the paltry paycheck his father hands him each Friday afternoon.

Besides, the thought of living with any of his friends makes him cringe. None of his three closest friends could even been considered roommate material. They are all slobs, interested only in online gaming and eating. The only other person he'd contemplated sharing space with was his ex-girlfriend, Jesse Parker, but that's out of the question.

A twinge of sadness at the mere thought of Jesse makes tears spring into his eyes. Wiping them away, he sighs. God, how he misses her the old Jesse, not the one she'd turned into. His high school sweetheart—a girl with long, thick honey-colored hair, quick smile, and ability to laugh and not take life seriously—Jesse had been the perfect girlfriend until the last few months of their senior year.

On a whim, feeling the pressure of being model-thin and whining constantly about her curvy hips and thighs, Jesse caved and took her first hit of meth. He tried to warn her of the dangers, but she ignored him, promising she would only do it long enough to lose fifteen pounds.

Beautiful, sweet, carefree Jesse lost way more than fifteen pounds. She nearly lost her life. He tried to help her stop using the shit, but she became a full-blown junkie in less than two months. Fearing she would overdose he risked their relationship and told her mom, hoping the combination of mother and chief of police would break through the haze of drugs inside Jesse's mind.

He had been dead wrong.

Jesse flew into a rage, calling him every foul word she could think of in the parking lot of the

Piggly Wiggly. At the top of her voice, she threatened to castrate him, among other vile, despicable things. He tried to calm her down and take her keys, aware she was flying high, but one solid kick from her foot to his groin left him in a crumpled heap on the pavement in the parking lot.

Less than a month later, after being grounded for weeks, Jesse disappeared in the middle of the night. His one and only girlfriend fled to northwest Arkansas, and it took over two years for her to resurface, which only happened after she was busted for shoplifting at a convenience store to feed her raging addiction.

Chief Parker had gone to retrieve Jesse from Fayetteville and immediately transported her to rehab. Turner went online and found Jesse's mug shot. When he saw the haunted eyes, sunken cheeks, and pale skin, he sat inside his room and cried for the first time since their breakup.

The blowout of their relationship and the knowledge Turner had "ratted" Jesse out, left him alone in the world of female companionship. Everyone in the tiny town knew what went down between them, and even though the general comments he'd heard were positive, girls shied away from him like he had the plague.

His dating life was not enhanced by the fact he is one of those men people pass on the street and never give a second glance. He hovers just under six feet and has mousy brown hair and eyes and a lithe build. Basically, the same description people give the police when a white guy commits a crime.

His label of rat overrides bland locks and leaves him a lonely, bored man before his time.

When a teenager, he blamed his woes on his parents, but after graduating high school, concluded that wasn't fair. He put himself in the situation all on his own. He wasn't dumb, he just wasn't motivated in school to study or try and obtain scholarships for college. The amount of time and effort to do so just didn't interest him. His mother used to call him flighty and artistic when he was younger, which was true. Drawing, painting, and designing graphics are the only things he can do with minimal effort.

Unfortunately, those skills wouldn't pay the bills, so he kept his hobbies to himself and preferred to hang with his friends rather than buckle down and study. Knowing he could work for his father seemed the best—and easiest—road to travel.

Now, he regrets the decision, but it ss too late to change.

Other than the discussions and preparations for "whatever shit this old world brings" (his dad's favorite saying around the dinner table), his home life is normal, if there really was such a thing. His parents are all about preparing for the end of the world and teaching Turner how to survive when society collapses, yet Walter and Martha Addison are good people. Honest. Well-respected throughout the community. They are typical southern Bible thumpers who love God and others, yet standoffish of big government.

Most of the time growing up, he tuned out his father's ramblings about disasters, world-wide plagues, lying governments, and a host of other, ridiculous conspiracy theories, however, during the last year, he started researching things on his own. At first, he hoped to find evidence on the Internet to prove his father was nuttier than Aunt Linda's Christmas fruitcake. A few sites he visited confirmed his ideas, yet most supported his father's.

The more news he watched, the more he grew to understand his father's strange ideas weren't too far from the mark. Shootings, bombings, diseases, wars, rumors of wars, people being beheaded simply over religion—it was like he finally woke up from the dream he'd been living in. The truth of the ugliness in the world slapped him out of the dazed fund and into reality.

Those things contributed to his change of heart, yet what truly swayed his opinion of the world came from Trevor Montgomery.

Trevor was the older brother of Seth Montgomery, one of his closest friends. After graduating high school, Trevor enlisted in the Army and completed two tours in Afghanistan. When Trevor returned home, he was nowhere near the person he'd been before. Seth said his brother suffered from PTSD, which was completely understandable given where he'd been stationed, yet it was the horror stories of what he'd witnessed while overseas that made Turner sit up and take notice.

Trevor didn't tell the stories directly to him. Seth retold the tales from countless nights sitting beside his brother, trying to talk him down as the panic attacks tore through his destroyed mind. The similarities to his father's sordid tales were astonishing, and Turner became a believer that no one—or government entity—could be trusted.

Period.

Glancing at the trail less than ten feet away, his heart thumps faster when settling on the footprints. Though he isn't quite convinced the imprints were made by someone from the government, they still make him feel edgy because all the years they'd tromped up and down the path to the cave, they'd never run across any.

Ever.

"No, stop it. This is ridiculous. They're just from another hunter, that's all. Some other redneck fool. Maybe one got lost after following the barks of a hound on the trail of a deer, pig, or some other kind of hairy critter."

The wind picks up, blowing dried leaves across the trail. A strange sense of fear causes him to shudder as the sensation of someone watching him makes his skin crawl. Unwilling to be a sitting duck, he stands and pulls out the Bowie knife from its sheath.

When his father's voice rings out, calling for him to come to the cave and that all is fine, he turns tail and runs as though the devil is right on his heels.

***

"How long does it take for the formula to work? What methods of administration have you tried?"

Everett is still riding on cloud nine from the discovery two days prior. He decides to ignore the snide tone of Dr. Jason Thomas.

The man had descended into the lab with an attitude of arrogance, which rubbed him the wrong way. Instead of showing even a modicum of enthusiasm or excitement at the discovery, Dr. Thomas appeared annoyed and full of doubt before anyone on the team even had a chance to show him the results. Everett hoped the man's negativity would change after the initial meeting and walk-through of the results over thirty-six hours ago, yet so far, Dr. Thomas remains skeptical.

While motioning toward the other cages perched on top of Ultima's, he takes a deep breath to steady his irritation before answering the questions. "Ultima received his dose via intramuscular injection. These two over here received theirs via the sublingual method. The next trial will be inhalation. Response time for each method so far varies between fifteen minutes and two hours for full effect."

"I see." Dr. Thomas's gaze lingers on each subject briefly and then he focuses his attention on Everett. "Are you also going to attempt oral administration or are you worried the chemical makeup of the formula will break down when formatted into capsule or tablet form?"

"Our plan is to watch and observe the four subjects for the next week before we attempt any other testing. So far, no adverse side effects have surfaced other than slight loss of appetite and low-grade fever. The fever lasted less than two hours in each mouse, and their interest in food is beginning to increase, albeit slower than what we'd like to see. I am confident the formula will not suffer any major chemical changes no matter what form is used to administer it."

"Agreed." Dr. Riverside adds. "Since we used transgenic bacteria as the basis, the method of delivery should not change the effectiveness of the formula."

Everett gives the kid a slight grin, appreciative for the support. "Exactly. Once the bacteria enter the brain, specifically, the nucleus accumbens, they attach to the neurotransmitters. Basically, when necessary, the bacteria release enzymes to regulate the dopamine levels in the brain, thus maintaining steady levels."

"What happens when something stimulates the cells to produce extra dopamine?" Dr. Thomas furrows his brows in disbelief. "Like when an orgasm is reached, or if more drugs are introduced into the body? How will this formula of yours stop the flood of dopamine?"

"May I answer this, Dr. Berning?"

Everett nods at Dr. Flint, who's been standing next to Dr. Thomas the entire time and seems eager to contribute. "Be my guest."

She turns and addresses Dr. Thomas. "Great question and one the three of us discussed numerous times. Dr. Berning is the genius who came up with the idea to use transgenic bacteria. He tweaked the DNA to detect high levels of dopamine. Orgasmic release is not affected since the intensity of dopamine isn't near the amounts triggered when narcotics enter the brain. When levels are normal, the bacteria remain dormant as an invisible coating overlaying the cells. However, when a particular level is reached, the bacteria reanimate and form a protective barrier around the neurotransmitters. Enzymes are released to attack and destroy the excess dopamine which is then eliminated from the body. After levels dip below a certain threshold, the bacteria return to dormancy."

"Fascinating," Dr. Thomas remarks. "How long do you project the bacteria will remain adhered to the cells?"

Everett blinks twice, shocked by the question. As a physician, Dr. Thomas should already know the answer. "As with all bacteria introduced into the body, as long as the T-cells don't create antibodies to destroy the bacteria, and no external antibiotics are administered, they will remain inside the host cells forever."

Dr. Thomas hands Everett the binder containing his notes, which he'd been studying ever since his arrival, requesting them first to focus on the research before viewing the full results in the mice. "Are you suggesting this discovery is a permanent cure for addiction? What happens when the addict is confronted with drugs? Will the enhanced bacteria keep them from succumbing to temptation and ingesting them?"

Everett smiles. This is the question he's been waiting for Dr. Thomas to ask. "Allow me to demonstrate."

Reaching inside Ultima's cage, he deposits a fresh pile of pure heroin into the food dish. The mouse didn't seem to notice. For dramatic effect, he grabs the mouse by the tail and drops Ultima on top of the heroin. The mouse scurries away to the opposite end of the cage without even a second glance at the drugs.

"See? No interest at all. Our hypothesis is the bacteria acts as a shield even when dormant, making the host uninterested in the drug."

Dr. Thomas moves past him and snatches up the mouse. "I would like to see what happens when accidental ingestion occurs."

Nodding in agreement, Everett picks up a syringe loaded with heroin. Taking Ultima from Dr. Thomas, he gives the mouse a small injection. The reaction is immediate. Ultima jerks, his tiny body rigid. Before Everett can deposit him back inside the cage, the mouse does the unthinkable: he vomits.

Dr. Thomas gasps. "What in the world? How is that even possible? Rodents don't have the capability to emesis."

Everett forces himself not to laugh. "And up until two days ago, there wasn't a cure for addiction."

The foursome falls silent while watching Ultima's strange reaction. Once the mouse stops vomiting, it returns to the far end of the cage and curls up into a ball.

Breaking the silence, Dr. Thomas lets out a low whistle. "Had I not seen this with my own eyes, I wouldn't have believed it. Okay, ladies and gentlemen. It's time to move to the next level."

"Are you saying we begin human trials already?" Dr. Riverside queries, the shock of the statement by Dr. Thomas seeping into the words. "If so, I must disagree. We have a lot of preliminary testing to complete first."

"Recall who is running this show, Dr. Riverside." Dr. Thomas holds up a gnarled hand. "We are wasting precious time arguing about trivial things. Lives are being lost by the thousands as we speak. The sooner the better. Twenty-five test subjects have already been chosen and will be here by tomorrow afternoon, so I suggest you all make appropriate preparations and calculations necessary to begin human trials by the end of the week. Good work, all."

All three watch Dr. Thomas turn and exit the lab. Each in shock, trying to grasp the magnitude of his instructions, it takes them several seconds to regain their faculties.

"You heard the man. Time to sink or swim," Dr. Flint instructs. "Dr. Berning, you start the calculations on body mass ratios for men and women. Dr. Riverside, come with me. We will start preparing the questionnaires and rooms for our guests."

Everett's mind spins at the news. "Human trials? Already? We aren't prepared! I haven't even finished all my notes, not to mention begun the arduous process of filling out the investigational new drug application for submittal to the CDER at the Food and Drug Administration. It will take, at a minimum, one month to complete. Even if I could extrapolate all the data necessary in record time, we still must wait thirty days for the FDA to review the lab results before they give us permission to continue clinical trials. This is preposterous!"

Dr. Flint bristles. "Everett, those issues are not what we need to be concerned about. I assure you Dr. Thomas will handle governmental issues. You concentrate your efforts on the tasks given."

"Guess the government gives more leeway to its own discoveries than corporations, huh?" Dr. Riverside interjects. "One of the perks of working for Uncle Sam, I suppose."

Everett clamps his mouth shut as he watches his two colleagues leave the lab. His excitement wanes as a sense of foreboding rolls around inside his chest. Once alone, he mutters, "This isn't right. Not right at all."

Chapter 4 - Ready to Roll

One Year Later - Tuesday, December 15th –
10:00 a.m.

EVERETT STARES AT THE YOUNG WOMAN
seated across the table. Susan Richmond is twenty-four and a former methamphetamine addict since the age of fifteen. The last three years of her life prior to arriving at the facility were spent living on the streets of Memphis, prostituting herself to feed an insatiable habit. Her arrest record is four pages long, consisting of drug charges, prostitution, and theft. After running away from home at seventeen, she lost contact with her family. During one of her court-ordered drug treatment stints, Susan reached out to her only living relative, her mother, only to discover she'd passed away six months prior. The sadness drove Susan to escape from the facility and seek out the drug that wiped out the overwhelming sorrow from her thoughts.

"How are you feeling today, Susan?"

"Fine. Ready to leave this dump."

Everett stares at the girl and suppresses a smile. Susan gained twenty pounds of healthy muscle since her arrival almost twelve months prior. The pale, gaunt-faced wisp of a girl is gone, replaced by a healthy-looking young lady. Susan's light brown hair is thick and shiny, her cheeks full and tinged with a hint of pink. The transformation is remarkable.

"As I mentioned yesterday, the clinical trial lasts a full year. Only one more week and then you'll be free to go. You signed up for a year, remember?"

Susan huffs. A look of annoyance and distrust glistens behind dark, brown eyes. "I shouldn't be held to agreements made when I was so strung out, I barely remembered my own name. I mean, it's not like I had much of a choice. The thug who brought me here scared the living shit out of me. One minute, I'm standing on the corner talking to a john and the next, knocked unconscious and wake up in the back of a van, hogtied and gagged. When he yanked me out, I saw the entrance to a cave, I thought I was a goner. To say I was terrified is an understatement. I signed on the dotted line only because I thought it would keep me alive."

Unable to hide his disgust at the girl's treatment even though he's heard her story many times, he reaches across the table and pats her hand. "As I've stated many times before, I am sorry your journey here was so disarming. It started out frightening, but I believe it turned out well for you. Agree?"

Susan moves her arm away and shifts in the seat, sighs once, and takes a sip of tea. "Yeah, now. Being clean and healthy hasn't stopped the nightmares about my so-called journey here. I suppose you will never understand, so I won't even try to explain."

"You're right. I can only sympathize with your emotions since I haven't experienced your situation. Let's get back to how you feel. Other than the nightmares, any other symptoms you need to report?"

"No. My appetite is fine. No headaches or cravings. No muscle cramps, body aches or fever.

Other than being a bit antsy to leave here, I feel fine."

"Excellent news. No interest at all in returning to the habits of your old life, correct?"

"None at all. Just the thought of even one hit makes me feel sick to my stomach. If I dwell on the idea too long, I throw up. Is that normal?"

He smiles. "Yes. The medication we administered to you is designed to trigger your brain to eschew any cravings for narcotics by making the recipient feel nauseated. As you are aware from earlier testing, if you ingest any type of drug, the reaction is quick and unpleasant."

"Yeah, haven't puked that hard since I had food poisoning when I was twelve." Susan crinkles her pert nose in disgust. "This cure of yours is amazing. Miraculous, even. Sorry about being so bitchy earlier. I am grateful for what you've done for me. Really. It's just, I'm ready to start living my new life."

"I know. One more week, I promise."

Her eyes fill with tears while staring at the cup on the table. "I really wish my mom was still alive. I caused her a lot of grief when I was using the shit. All she ever wanted out of life was to see me clean. Now, it's too late. Will it do me any good to ask again exactly what you gave me? Or where I am?"

"Only if your goal is to hear the same answer again." Everett stands, gathers up the notebook and coffee mug. "But it's not too late for you to start a new, drug-free lifestyle. I recall you mentioned in one of our earlier discussions you once considered being a nurse as your calling. Perhaps it is time to examine that desire more closely. You will have plenty of cash to live off for at least two years once you leave here."

"Fifty thousand dollars for a year of my life is generous, no doubt. But living off that amount, after taxes, won't stretch into two years. I'm afraid college is out of the question for me. I still must get my GED…"

He pauses at the door, feigning a look of shock. The moment he's been waiting for to break the good news just presented itself. "Oh, did I forget to explain the college scholarship portion of your package?"

Susan's mouth drops open. "Come again?"

"Guess I neglected that section. Sorry. Yes, as a thank you for helping us, we've already secured a scholarship at Emory University in Atlanta. Barring any sudden side effects from your treatment, you are scheduled to begin classes at the Nell Hodgson Woodruff School of Nursing when the spring semester begins."

"What? No way! I don't even have my GED yet. I haven't applied…and I can't afford to live in Atlanta. I have nothing. No clothes, no car, and certainly no knowledge of the area. Are you just going to hand me all this and then dump me off? Alone? I'll freak!"

Motioning for Susan to follow, he holds the door open. "Ma'am, I assure you all has been taken care of. These perks are our way of thanking you for your time and service to the project. Think of it as one big eraser. Your old life is wiped away, and a door to the new one just opened. It's as simple as that. And don't worry, you won't be alone."

"I won't?"

He stops in front of a set of sealed doors. After unlocking them, he ushers her inside. Twenty-four other heads turned their direction, some smiling, some emotionless.

"Susan, I would like to introduce you to the other participants in our trials. Each of them has similar stories to your own, and their reactions to the formula are just as impressive. Diane here will be your roommate in Atlanta. She's also enrolled in the nursing course."

A tall, red-headed woman rises and walks across the concrete floor. She extends her hand. "Nice to meet you, Susan. I'm Diane Rogers. Come on, have a seat before you pass out. I almost did when Dr. Berning brought me here earlier. Finding out you weren't alone in all this is quite a jolt to the system, huh?"

"Jolt? Uh, try bolt of lightning to the brain."

"Susan is our last guest to arrive, so please get acquainted with one another. Lunch will be served shortly. Oh, and congratulations everyone on completing the program."

Without another word, Everett exits the large meeting room as all the participants stand and introduce themselves to the freaked-out Susan.

Lost in thought about finalizing reports, awash in excitement at the knowledge they were only days away from announcing the cure to the general public, Everett never hears the footsteps behind him.

Until it is too late.

***

Regine smiles while adjusting the vest underneath her uniform. The sound of banter between Reed and Jesse in the living room is glorious. Reed is doing his best to convince his niece he is a better shot than Regina, and Jesse is having none of it.

"I've been to the shooting range with Mom so many times I've lost count. She outshoots all competitors every time. Women have a steadier hand, plain and simple. She'd whoop your ass, Uncle Reed."

"Care to put your money where your smart-assed mouth is?"

"Name the time and place. I have every confidence in Mom."

Shaking her head, Regina veers off into the kitchen to fix a cup of coffee before heading to the station. After dousing the cup with more creamer than coffee, she joins the arguing duo in the living room.

"Enough, you two. Jesse, are you ready for work? I'll drop you off on my way."

"Mom, Uncle Reed thinks he's a better shot than you. When's your next day off? We need to have a shootout. I've got a week's worth of pay riding on you!"

"No time to talk about that now, Jesse. Your shift at Walmart starts in fifteen minutes. You aren't even dressed yet."

"That sounds like an excuse to me. Worried your daughter is wrong, sis?"

Regina scowls at Reed. "Not at all. Sunday is my next day off, so you're on. High noon, brother. Now, Jesse, hurry up!"

"Yes!" Jesse chirps as she rises from the couch and jogs down the hallway toward her room. "Don't worry about taking me, Mom. Turner's picking me up."

Before Regina can respond, Jesse disappears inside her room. She takes a sip of coffee and grins at Reed. "What a turnaround, huh?"

"No doubt." He nods while returning the smile. "Seeing her healthy, clean, and full of life is a true Christmas blessing. She's a completely different girl than the one a year ago. Always knew she was an amazing gal. Just like her mom."

"And uncle. After all, you were instrumental in keeping the two of us from ripping each other apart once she came home from rehab. Lord, those first few months were awful."

Reed stands and grabs her jacket from the chair, laughing as he hands it to her. "No kidding. It was like trying to separate two wet cats. You both have horrible tempers. That trait came from Dad. I'm more of a peacemaker, like Mom."

Sliding the jacket on, she snorts. "You have a lot of her traits, including her inability to shoot the side of a barn."

"Oh, did you just toss the gauntlet of challenge at my feet?"

"Yep. You may be taller and more of a peacemaker than I am, yet I will school you at target practice, just like when we were kids. Some things don't change over the years. My besting you with a gun is one of them."

A car horn beeps, followed by Jesse bursting from her room. "Turner's picking me up after work and we're going to shop for gifts. Have a good shift, Mom. Love you."

Regina bristles. "Jesse, I don't think that's a good idea."

"Stop worrying, Mom. I'm done with my old life, I promise. We're going to buy gifts then come right back here to wrap them, I swear."

Biting her lip before saying something that would spark an argument, Regina remains silent while Jesse kisses her cheek. In a flash, she is out the door.

Reed's warm arm wraps around her shoulder. "Let it go, Sis. She's fine. Turner Addison is a good influence on her. You can't expect her to spend all her time at work and this house. Girl's gotta have a life—and learn to live it sober."

"The cop in me knows that. The mother in me doesn't."

With a fatherly pat, Reed pushes her toward the front door. "The mother in you seems to forget about the ace in the hole: me. Jesse hasn't figured out yet I'm tracking her every move. Now go, concentrate on keeping the peace in Rockport from crazy rednecks. I've got your back, as always."

Regina nods and leaves the house, thankful for her daughter's sobriety and her brother's presence.

***

Benito finishes breakfast and stares out across the vast expanse of what is now his estate. He picks up the notebook to his right and thumbs through the pages, again, going over every detail of the year's transactions. Satisfied he is on track with the goals he'd set out for himself two years prior, he lets a small grin appear.

"Good morning, my love. My, but you seem especially happy this morning. Do I dare hope it is because of the way I woke you up earlier?"

Maria's sweet voice from behind him makes his dick hard. The woman is sexier than any woman he'd ever met; beauty only matched in intensity by her abilities between the sheets.

He reaches around the chair, grabbing a handful of her full ass. "Si, my treasure. You always make me happy. However, you cannot take all the credit for my mood today. It is almost Christmas, and I was just going over the books for the year. Things are so profitable I am having trouble deciding what extravagant present to give you. Any ideas you'd like to share?"

Maria squeals and jumps into Benito's lap. "Si, mi cielo. Other than your undying love, I only wish for two things."

He nuzzles her soft neck. "And they are?"

Maria groans while grinding her hips in his lap. "Fuller breasts and the ability to say they were a gift from my future husband. I want to be at my best for Teresa's wedding next December. It will be my first trip to the United States, and I want everything to be perfect, and for everyone to want to be me, including my sister."

"Ah, you wish to be my wife?" He whispers before nipping the soft flesh of her neck. "What a coincidence. That was my Christmas wish as well, and why I bought this."

He extracts a small black box from his pocket.

Maria's eyes widen and she claps her hands like a little girl. Her fingers shake as she opens the box, revealing a twenty-two carat, princess cut ring nestled inside the white satin.

She is so excited it takes her two tries to slide the ring onto her finger. "Mi cielo! Oh, it's beautiful!"

"As are you, my love. Now, about your other wish: I disagree." He pulls down the silk blouse from her shoulders with his teeth, exposing her perky breast, letting his tongue slide around the nipple twice before sucking. "These beauties are perfect the way they are. I don't understand why you want to change them."

Maria moans again while jutting her chest forward. "I will give you all the pleasure you desire, mi cielo, more than I am capable of now, if you allow me this indulgence. It will make me feel more in proportion—and much sexier."

"Whatever you wish, my love." He wraps his arms around her firm rump and hefts her off his lap. Then, as usual, he takes the daughter of the man whose life he ended into the bedroom and violates every inch of her body.

When reflecting on the moment later, after the phone call that changed everything, Benito would realize the defilement of Mario Alvarado's daughter was the final time things worked in his favor.

***

"If this is some sort of joke, I assure you that you will regret playing it on me."

"No, sir. You wanted me to report on all the new developments, and this is where we are now. It is ready. The formula passed all the trials with flying colors. The test subjects will be released by week's end. The team is nearly finished with all the paperwork and a press conference scheduled for next week. I don't have the exact time or location yet, but I assure you when I do, I will let you know."

Benito forces himself to remain calm. He knew this day would come and had been preparing on his end ever since the night of his birthday, when he opened the safe and discovered Mario's secret.

That night, after reading through all of Mario's notes, he'd been surprised he agreed with the prick's conclusions, which was not to let the atrocity happen. Of course, his reasoning was far different than Mario's.

The discovery would ruin Benito's new livelihood. A permanent cure for drug addiction would wipe out his business and thousands of others around the globe. Economies would be devastated when drugs quit flowing.

Ever since he'd been alerted to the possibility of the cure, he'd worked nonstop, risking his life numerous times by setting up meetings with local competitors and other cartel warlords across the globe. Only a few rejected his proposal to band together to keep the concoction from hitting the streets. Most were on board when he gave them a demonstration of the cure's abilities.

Benito suffered too many years of abuse to walk away from the lifestyle he'd stolen from Mario. Living a life of luxury, banging the sick bastard's daughter, and owning the massive estate were his rewards for being tortured by the fat slob. There is no way he'd give up the prizes he'd earned from every vile, disgusting moment he'd endured for almost twelve years.

Shaking the thoughts away, he takes in a gulp of air. "No, you will make sure the press conference never happens. If it is as you say, then proceed with the plans we set out. Make sure nothing—and no one—remains. Only bring our little friend to see me. He will turn out to be quite useful, I believe. After all, what better asset could I ask for than forcing the man who created this nightmare to atone for his mistakes by creating the world's most addictive drugs known to man? He is to arrive here without one hair out of place and the cure he created in one piece. Can't create an antidote unless we have the sickness. Understood?"

"As you wish, sir." The voice on the other end of the line is cold, harsh. "Consider it done. I will contact you on the new number once everything is completed."

The line goes dead. Benito stares at the blank screen of his cell before tearing the phone apart and throwing the remains into the fireplace. While he watches the plastic melt, he dreads the next calls he needs to make. The other businessmen will be just as nervous and disturbed about the turn of events as he is because all of them know the gravity of the situation if his contact inside the laboratory fails them.

Opening the drawer of the massive wooden desk, he extracts fifteen disposable phones. One by one, he makes the calls to others in similar positions to his own around the world, dropping the latest, unsettling news into their ears and then assuring them his next phone call will be full of good news.

Chapter 5 - Starting Over

Wednesday, December 16th – 4:00 a.m.

THE THROBBING AT THE BACK OF Everett's head feels like someone running a jackhammer inside his skull. Disoriented, he tries to make sense of the sensory overload bombarding his mind. A weird, unfamiliar sound drums in his head. It takes several seconds for him to figure out the noise ss the rhythmic hum of tires on the open road. Coupled with the motion of riding inside a vehicle, the knowledge makes his head spin. A vehicle? How? The lab is underground, and he doesn't recall leaving.

Then again, he cannot remember a thing after leaving Susan and the other test subjects inside the meeting room.

What the hell is going on?

Nothing makes sense, so he concludes he must be asleep in his quarters, dreaming.

He hears someone speaking in quick yet hushed tones. The sound of the muffled, male voice seems to be coming from all around him. He forces his mind to slow down and home in on the words.

"Repeating…the White House just confirmed First Lady Roxanne Thompson succumbed to ovarian cancer less than an hour ago. President Thompson will give a press conference at nine a.m. Eastern Standard Time. Our thoughts and condolences go out to the President and his daughter Melissa during this trying time, especially with Christmas less than a week away. As we reported earlier, the first lady was battling the disease for several months now and..."

Sadness wells up inside his chest. He'd been keeping up with the first lady's fight against cancer online when he had down time. Hearing the news report makes his fuzzy brain aware he wasn't dreaming. He opens his burning eyes and is greeted by darkness and a faint tinge of neon green not far away. Mind still on the fritz, it takes him a few seconds to recognize the glow from a dashboard.

"You're awake? Oh, thank goodness! I was afraid you might have suffered permanent damage. You took a nasty blow to the head. Pretty sure you need stitches, but I didn't have time to patch you up. Too much was going on. Getting you to safety was my main priority."

Everett feels a rush of relief at the sound of Riverside's familiar voice. Forcing his body to move, he sits upright in the seat while touching the knot on the back of his head. The lump is the size of a walnut, and he feels a two-inch gash. When he pulls his hand away, the fingers are wet with blood. "Want to tell me what the hell is going on?"

Daryl turns down the radio before responding. "Not sure where to even start, Dr. Berning. I'm still not quite sure myself."

"Gee, that's helpful. Okay, how about explaining why it feels like someone whacked me with a two-by-four, and where we're going. I'll formulate more questions after you answer those."

"It was from the floor."

"What?"

"The bump on your head. You got it when you hit the floor."

Everett closes his eyes and rubs his temples. "Are you trying to tell me I passed out and you're taking me to the hospital or something?"

Riverside chuckles, but the sound is anything but humorous. "No. After Dr. Flint put you in a chokehold and you passed out, she let go and you fell onto the floor. Your head bounced off the concrete like a ripe watermelon. The sound was disgusting."

The memory of walking down the hallway flashes by inside head. He looks out the window into the darkness. "Dr. Flint did what? Why in the world would she do such a thing?"

Riverside lets off the gas and pulls over to the shoulder, puts the truck in park, and turns around. "Your guess is as good as mine. All I know is that I was coming out of the lab and saw her attack you. I didn't have a chance to ask what was going on because just as you hit the floor, the alarm went off, followed by screaming from all the test subjects in the conference room. Dr. Flint ran in the opposite direction the second the power went out. By the time the backup generator kicked in, she was gone. Then, I smelled smoke and felt the ground shake. I grabbed you, flung you over my shoulder and took the stairs until I reached the surface."

"Are you saying there was an explosion of some sorts? What about the others? Whose vehicle is this?"

Riverside tries to hide the fact he is shaking but it is no use. "It would only be an educated guess to say there was an explosion. I didn't see any fire, nor was there any structural damage, at least none I could see. I just felt the rattle—you know—like the whole place was going to collapse, so I grabbed you, my backpack, and took us to safety. Not a clue as to the owner of the truck, and honestly, I don't care. Lucky for us the keys were inside, so I tossed you in the back and waited for a few minutes to see if anyone else made it out. When no one came out the door, I took off. Just as I started up the vehicle, I heard another rumble and smoke billowed out the front entrance."

Everett looks out the window again. Nothing but dense woods as far as he can see surround them. The trees and terrain are unfamiliar. "How long have you been driving?"

"About ten hours."

"Holy shit! Where in the hell are we?"

"Close to Laredo. I think about twenty miles out."

"Laredo…as in…Laredo, Texas?"

Daryl nods before taking a deep breath. "Look, I don't really know how to say this so I'll just this, it out. I'm pretty sure the lab is gone. It sounded like the cave was about to collapse when I was hauling you up the stairs. Judging by what I found out before running into you in the hallway, I'd lay my life down on the bet the incident was from internal sabotage."

He blinks twice, trying to absorb the shocking words. "Are you saying you think Dr. Flint destroyed all our work? Killed our test subjects? Why in the world would she do that? What about

Dr. Thomas? Did you see him? Did he make it out? Oh, and did you contact the authorities? Are they sending backup?"

"I don't know about anyone but us. And yes, I'm saying Dr. Flint did all this. In terms of backup, you are kidding, right?"

"No, I'm not kidding. You didn't call anyone and inform them what happened?"

The look of incredulity on Daryl's face would be funny under other circumstances. The kid gapes at him like he just asked the stupidest question ever.

Daryl arches an inquisitive eyebrow. "Wait, you're serious? Oh, man, you really don't have a clue, do you? No, I guess you wouldn't. You've been too obsessed with your work."

Frustrated from the pain in his head and the feeling of walking in the dark on jagged rocks, he shakes his head.

"We haven't been working for any government entity, Dr. Berning." Riverside let out a long sigh. "This whole project consisted of me, you, Dr. Flint, and Dr. Thomas. All funded and put together covertly by one individual: Dr. Thomas."

A wave of dizziness sweeps over Everett at the news. How in the hell was he so easily duped? "That's going to take a minute for me to digest. Okay, okay. So, we were on our own. Let's get back to what you found out before you rescued me."

Leaning across the seat. Daryl grabs a bag resting on the passenger side, open it up, and retrieves several sheets of crinkled paper. "I overheard Dr. Flint talking to someone on the phone in her office about two hours before all this happened. She didn't know I was at her door since her back was to me. I have no clue who she was talking to, but I did get the gist of their conversation. None of it was good for us. I was going to come find you first, but figured you wouldn't believe me without proof, so I went back to the lab and hacked into her email account and found these."

Everett reaches out to grab the handful of papers but stops short. An overwhelming sense of fear ambles up his spine. The thought of turning the interior light on makes his stomach clench as paranoia roils inside his brain. "Just tell me the specifics of the communications, Riverside."

"These are email exchanges between Dr. Flint, and someone named B.S.N. They go all the way back to the day after the discovery last year. Discussions about the cure, how the test subjects reacted to treatment, everything. I only heard her side of the conversation, but it was apparent she was to shut down the operation, get rid of the formula and evidence, including us, and leave before we had a chance to share the discovery with the press next week."

The air leaves his lungs in a giant whoosh. The throbbing in his head is a fleeting memory, overshadowed by raw terror thrumming inside his chest. "Oh, my God. What about the formula? Please don't tell me all our hard work is lost!"

"Don't worry, I've got five full vials right here." Riverside smiles for the first time during their conversation while patting the bag on the seat. "I also have a flash drive containing all of our notes on formula 10,899. The lab may be gone, but our work isn't. Even if we lost the vials, we could simply create a new batch."

He must quell the anxiety inside his mind, so he takes a deep breath, shoving the paralyzing fear down deep and counts to ten. "Okay, let me think for a minute. What time is it?"

"A little after four a.m."

"And we're almost to Laredo, correct? You've been driving the entire time?"

"Yes. Only stopped twice for gas."

"So, where was our starting point?"

Riverside snickers. "You don't know?"

Everett shakes his head.

"Wow, all these years you've worked at the lab and had no clue where you were?"

"I was busy doing research, Daryl." He snaps, irritation creeping into his voice. "Trivial things like my location didn't rank high enough on my priority list. Where did we come from?"

"Arkansas. The lab was underground in the Ozark Mountains about fifty miles south of Blanchard Springs Caverns, to be exact."

"I've been in Arkansas all this time. Unreal."

For a few minutes, neither man speaks. Everett's head thumps in time with each heartbeat. He feels lightheaded from lack of food and water. "Please tell me we at least have some water."

Daryl bends forward, fumbling underneath the seat until producing a plastic bottle. He passes it back to Everett, and though he wants to gulp down the entire sixteen ounces, he only took a few sips.

Just like the day he found out his entire family died, a dark cloak of uncertainty drapes over his mind and heart. The implications of what Riverside said are almost too much for his brain to comprehend.

He takes one last drink and twists the cap back on. "Okay, son. Guess it's just you and me for the moment. First, thank you for saving my life—and our work. Secondly, tell me why in the hell we're heading to Laredo. Thirdly, do so while driving. The thought of staying stationary makes me uncomfortable."

Riverside starts up the truck. In seconds, the road whizzes by in a blurred rush as they pass a sign welcoming them to Webb County, Texas.

Clearing his throat, Riverside finally answers the question. "Figured both of our homes weren't safe choices, you know, because we really don't have a clue who's behind all this. My uncle died last year and left me a cabin outside of Laredo near the Mexican border. Only my family knows about the place, and, well, technically he wasn't my uncle. He was really my mother's ex-boyfriend, but we stayed in touch over the years. He never married or had any kids, so he left what he had to me. If my gut feeling is right—which it usually is—the government is behind all this, so they'll be searching for us once they realize we made it out alive. We might not be able to stay at the cabin long, but at least maybe enough time to gather ourselves together and form a workable plan."

He considers arguing with the kid because he currently doesn't have the mental faculties to formulate a better plan of action, yet a nagging sense of distrust rumbles around in his mind. It takes a few minutes to pinpoint the reason as thoughts race at a blistering pace.

The time.

That's what is bothering him. Nearly twenty-four hours had passed since he left Susan and the others. Even though he is a few months' shy of turning sixty-five, he is in good health. There is no way a bump on the head would have rendered him unconscious for such a long period of time. He had to have been drugged—so who in the hell drugged him?

The realization increases the distrust and unease burning inside his stomach and chest.

Without all the real facts to review, it is impossible for him to know if he should trust anyone at this point, even Riverside.

He swallows hard and makes sure his voice is strong and steady. "Fine. Just stay under the speed limit and adhere to all traffic laws. By now, this vehicle is probably listed as stolen."

Chapter 6 - Showdown in Laredo

Friday, December 18th – 10:00 p.m.

THE TWO-ROOM CABIN IS SITUATED on a small rise overlooking the Rio Grande. The arid, open landscape is full of short, scrubby plants that look more like bushes than trees. The sparse scenery does nothing to help quell Everett's fears of being discovered.

Ever since their arrival two days prior, he has been on constant edge. Rather than sleep, he takes catnaps lasting less than an hour. He is exhausted physically yet his mind refuses to shut down.

Daryl tries his best to make him comfortable, answering all the rapid-fire questions he throws at him with his usual flair for humor. Though aware the young doctor is probably trying to help ease his worried mind, the casual way the kid answers the questions sets his nerves on edge.

He faked falling asleep earlier on the bed, waiting for his companion to do the same. His plan was to hold still until Daryl fell into deep REM sleep and then snatch the keys and backpack. Doubt festered inside his mind about his roomie's true motives until he couldn't stand another minute locked inside the cabin.

The first inkling something was amiss happened inside the truck on the way to the cabin. The second one arrived when they settled themselves inside the dusty place and Everett asked to read the emails purportedly from Dr. Flint. Daryl agreed, but kept requesting help settling in first. After locating the candles, checking for snakes, and unloading the truck, Everett asked again, and Daryl said to wait until he used the bathroom so they could go over them together.

While waiting for him to relieve his bladder and bowels, Everett sat down to catch his breath and promptly fell asleep. When he woke up less than two hours later, he damn near pissed himself when he realized he was alone. Three hours later, Daryl returned with an armful of groceries.

Once the supplies were stowed away, he requested the pages again, yet Riverside changed the subject and started talking about what happened while cleaning and bandaging Everett's head. Riverside was dodging the requests, and it was the final straw severing his trust. Everett hadn't asked about the emails again, opting to grill the kid for as much information as possible about other circumstances regarding their escape, pretending the injury to his head caused him to forget important details.

A lone coyote howls outside, making the hairs stand erect on his arms. He pushes the eerie noise aside and concentrates on Riverside's respirations. Sweat pools under his armpits and on his brow while staring at a stained spot on the ceiling. Never, in his whole life, had Everett ever been the kind of man one would consider stealthy, deceitful, or capable of violence. His precious, sweet wife, Carol, used to tease him, calling him her gentle teddy bear.

He'd given serious consideration to confronting the man he now considers his captor physically since they were close to the same height and weight, but the thirty-year age span doesn't work in his favor. Instead, he stole peeks around the cabin in search of a weapon to balance out the gap, yet the only thing he noticed in plain sight was a set of steak knives on the counter, and he dismissed the idea of grabbing one the second the idea popped into his mind.

Everett is a typical nerdy scientist, one holding dual degrees in both microbiology and chemistry. Other than testing animals at laboratories—and only done so to confirm results—he'd never physically harmed another living creature. The sad truth is he doesn't possess the skills to carry out a mental plan to overpower, and possibly kill, his former colleague.

The only other option available to craft an escape was stealth. Tonight, he had no choice except to embrace the darker side of his personality if he planned on making it out of the cabin, and Texas, alive. His gut instincts warned the clock was ticking precious seconds away, counting down until his time breathing air ceased.

With slow, calculated movements, he inches his body into the sitting position, wincing while holding his breath as the old wood underneath the mattress creaks. Vision already accustomed to the dark interior, he scans the entire space, which wasn't more than six-hundred square feet, pausing to ensure the kid is still out. His gaze settles on the strap of the backpack poking out from underneath the bunk Daryl is stretched out on, fast asleep, and the keys clipped onto a hook on the bottom of the satchel.

He's already calculated how many steps it will take to reach the bag then exit the cabin. The front door hinges are in desperate need of oil and make tremendous racket when opened, so he opted to slip out the window next to his bunk. Each time Daryl had stepped into the restroom or went outside to retrieve something from the truck, Everett inched the window open a bit further. Only a few more inches and he can slip through with ease.

Without taking his focus off Riverside, he stands and stretches his arms across the expanse of the bed. His fingers find the window. Taking in a deep breath to steady his hands, he pushes the pane all the way open.

Riverside never moves or changes his respirations.

Nervous sweat drips into his eyes, making them burn. Just as he reaches up to wipe his sticky brow, movement to the right catches his attention. Heart pounding, Everett drops into a crouch and squints out the window. His mouth goes dry when seeing headlights shimmer in the distance, and someone standing less than twenty feet from the window. His heartrate spikes upon noticing the unmistakable shape of an automatic weapon illuminated by the light of the silvery moon's rays.

He hears the vehicle's engine now, and apparently, so does the intruder outside. The body drops into a crouch, out of his line of sight.

Terror keeps his mouth clamped shut as he crouches and crawls across the dirty wood floor over to Daryl's bed. For a split second, he considers not waking the kid up and warning him things are about to get ugly, but the fleeting thought leaves as quickly as it appears. He isn't wired that way, and even if Riverside is hiding something from him, he cannot leave him alone and helpless.

Finally next to the bed, he reaches up and clamps a hand over Riverside's mouth. "Daryl, wake up. We're in trouble. Don't say a word. Someone is outside, armed, and a vehicle is approaching at a high rate of speed."

Riverside's eyes fly open at the same moment his body jerks awake. He locks gazes with Everett, nods once, and then reaches a hand down and grabs the bag.

"Come on, we can go out back. On the count of three." Everett whispers.

Rather than panic and jump from the bed, Riverside bends over and laces up his tennis shoes. Stunned by the slow movements, Everett stares at the kid, mouth agape from shock. He wonders if Riverside is fully awake or still experiencing some sort of sleep-induced funk.

The sound of the engine roaring toward them grows louder. The headlights bathe the interior of the cabin in bright, white light, illuminating Riverside's face and to his disbelief, Everett notices the kid is grinning from ear to ear.

He knows now his gut instincts about Dr. Daryl Riverside were right on target.

"Get up, Dr. Berning. Our ride is here. Don't worry, they aren't going to harm you. Well, at least not if you follow their instructions. Veer from them, or try something stupid like running away, then all bets are off."

There is no way Everett will leave the world on all fours like a coward. He stands and wipes the dust from his jeans and shirt. "It was you, wasn't it? Not Dr. Flint."

"Yep. Life's all about the Bennies, Dr. Berning. All about the Bennies."

"The what?"

Riverside stands and jerks the pack over his shoulder. "Money you fool. You have no idea how glad I am this is over! God, I was so sick of being stuck in both hellholes with you. I gave up five years of my life waiting for this moment. Ten million dollars seemed like a tremendous amount at the time, but considering the mental anguish I suffered while underground, I think I will negotiate for more."

Instead of feeling terrified, Everett is livid. "You piece of shit! You killed them all, wasted all your talents to help your fellow man *for money*? Now I know why you picked this location. You're working with some cartel, aren't you? Has this been your plan all along?"

Daryl laughs while moving across the floor to the front door and unclipping the keys from the pack. He unlocks the door. "Yep. Oh, and handing you over to them was part of the deal, too. I mean, they couldn't turn down the opportunity to have the man who *almost* eradicated addiction on their team.

You'll be working for them now, just not in the capacity you'd expect. They plan on having you—"

The treacherous bastard never has the chance to finish the words when a bullet rips through the front door and tears open the right side of the boy's face before Everett really comprehended the sound of the rifle. Riverside's body flies back nearly five feet before crumpling onto the ground at the same time the door bursts open.

A large man dressed in black from head-to-toe crouches down and jerks the keys from Daryl's dead corpse. "If you don't want the assholes coming up the road to do the same to you, follow me. Now."

Everett is cornered and knows he has no choice but to comply. He doesn't look at Daryl's body on the floor as he runs past, yet he pauses to snatch up the bag with the formula. A strong arm yanks him away and shoves him out the front door toward the passenger side of the truck he'd arrived in with Daryl. The man who just saved his life tosses his gun and bag onto the floor before firing up the truck. The sound of pinging metal bounce all around.

"Hurry! Those ain't bees they're bullets!"

Yanking the door open, Everett leaps inside at the same time a bullet tears through his calf muscle. He screams in agony yet manages to get his entire body inside and shuts the door.

"Hang on."

In a haze of pain and shock, Everett yanks off his shirt and uses it as a tourniquet over the oozing wound in his leg. The truck bounces and bumps its way through the uneven terrain. Once his leg is secure, he turns and looks out the back window, thankful the nameless driver has outmaneuvered the vehicle behind them. From the rumbles of the engine, he can tell the man is pushing the Dodge to its limit.

Unwilling to interrupt the man's concentration on the task at hand, he remains silent while watching the headlights fade into the distance. In minutes, the view out the back window is black.

As the adrenaline rush wears off, a wave of dizziness makes the interior of the truck spin. To keep his mind engaged, Everett asks, "I'd sort of like to know the name of the man who just either saved my life or is the next one in line trying to end it. You know, so I can know who to come back and haunt after I'm dead or name my next kid after, whichever way this crazy night turns out."

Without taking his gaze off the road, the man grumbles, "You don't recognize me, Dr. Berning? Wow, I'm crushed."

Stunned, Everett leans over, peering closer. He recognizes the deep baritone voice, and confirmation he is correct is made by the green light of the dashboard. Though it had been months since the last time they'd met in person, the man's distinctive voice gave him away.

A verbal explosion of questions tumbles from his mouth. "Dirk Kincanon? Holy shit! Did Dr. Thomas send you? Please confirm he is okay. What about Dr. Flint and all those poor people inside the lab? How in the world did you find us?"

"GPS."

"Huh, oh, you mean on the truck?"

"Yes. When I couldn't reach Dr. Thomas, I located his vehicle. I knew things went sour when it showed up in Texas. Rest, Dr. Berning. Tend to your leg. There's a medical kit inside my bag. Get yourself patched up properly and let me get us out of this fucking state. Then we'll talk."

The sense of dread that had been Everett's constant companion for the last two days intensifies. He rifles through the bag resting on the floorboard, grateful the wound is to his calf muscle and not a major organ.

"One more question and then I promise I'll be quiet. Where are we going?"

The strong jaw line on Dirk's face flexes with irritation. "Arkansas, of course. The estate of Dr. Jason Thomas to be exact. It's too risky to head back to the lab right now. I don't know exactly how much Riverside told his partners."

Everett lets out a small sigh of relief. "The lab's intact?"

Dirk glances over and a snide grin appears. "You just asked another question."

"Can you blame me? I feel like I've been transported to an alternate reality. Knocked unconscious, kidnapped, almost killed—that's just the short list of fucked-up shit on my plate. Oh, and my leg is throbbing. I believe I'm suffering from a massive case of shock. Cut me some slack, will you?"

"Sit back and try to relax. We'll head to the lab once I'm sure it's safe to do so. In the meantime, we'll hunker down at Dr. Thomas' place. It's a fortress. We'll be safe there. I assure you no one gets inside unless I want them to."

A lump of tears gathers inside his dry throat because he has the answers to his questions about Dr. Thomas and the others. Dirk doesn't need to spell out the fact all the others are dead. Instead of succumbing to the emotions of the situation, he bends down and concentrates on binding his leg, fighting the urge to laugh out loud at the absurdity of the notion he will forever carry a scar from being shot.

He still cannot fathom he'd been in Arkansas for the last eleven years; completely oblivious he'd been less than one hundred miles from his small spread in the outskirts of Little Rock. Adding the latest new tidbits to the pile of other thoughts inside his mind from the events of the past year, he's surprised he hadn't suffered a psychotic break.

Unbelievable.

Chapter 7 - The End Begins

Present Day - Thursday, December 18th – 10:00
p.m.

MARIA ALVARADO'S huge new breasts are still tender after the surgery two weeks prior. Though sitting in first class, the flight from San Salvador to Phoenix has been full of turbulence, and all the shaking and bumping made her chest ache.

The throbbing pain she'd endured from the minute she awoke in her bedroom up until today was well worth the transformation. When she looked at herself in the mirror the first time after the bandages were removed, she saw the body of a real woman in the reflection. Finally, the bubbles on the backside had a matching set in the front.

Shifting in the seat, she stares out the window. The trip was her first airplane ride and taste of real freedom. When she first boarded, a fleeting thought of never returning danced inside her mind but knowing she would be hunted down like a lost pet, she quickly dismissed the idea.

The plane starts its descent into Phoenix. Lights twinkled below as far as she could see. The excitement of reuniting with her sister, showing off the rock on her finger, and newly acquired breasts, makes her giddy. Though they talk often on the phone, they hadn't seen each other since their father's murder two years prior. Teresa had flown to San Salvador, attended the funeral, and then stayed an entire week—long enough to witness their papa's killer die for his crime at the end of a rope in the stables. Since Teresa is the older sister, Benito allowed her to be the one to pull the lever.

Though rarely discussed, both sisters know exactly what their father and future husbands do for a living. They each like to refer to themselves as businessmen, but the Alvarado girls both knew what the term really means. Their father attempted to shelter them from the truth, keeping them away from the ugliness of his world, yet failed.

Teresa and Maria Alvarado are fully aware they are the children of El Salvador's biggest drug dealer. They grew up in the lap of luxury, no expense spared, or request denied. Their mother died giving birth to Maria, so she grew up surrounded by men. Her only interactions with females came from Teresa and the teachers brought in to provide both girls with an education. The flip side of being borne into privilege was neither of them ever went anywhere without bodyguards on the sprawling, twenty-five-thousand-acre grounds.

All was fine until Teresa fell in love with one of their father's lieutenants, Roberto Sanchez. Neither girl had ever left the estate and lived a blissful, naïve existence until the love bug bit her sister. Teresa drove their father crazy with her requests to follow Roberto to Phoenix, eventually threatening to kill herself if Roberto left without her.

Benito was instrumental in convincing their father to concede defeat. Mario Alvarado hated to lose, so to save face, he agreed as long as one condition was met: Teresa had to give up her heirship to his fortune and let it pass on to Maria.

Blinded by love, Teresa eagerly agreed and a few weeks later, she and Roberto left for Arizona.

Maria had been only seventeen and naively assumed Benito grasped the concept of love at all costs, sacrificing anything, including one's life and rightful ties to a family fortune, to be loved. While listening to the heartfelt speech Benito gave to their father, she felt herself fall head-over-heels for the boy. Up until then, she'd always considered Benito San Nicholas nothing more than an adoptive brother who had previously lived as common street trash— a boy rescued by their father on a whim one afternoon while in San Salvador conducting business.

Not long after Teresa left the estate, Maria set her sights on snagging Benito. At first, he remained distant, ignoring her brash advances. She grew angry and confronted him one night, insisting on knowing why he found her so undesirable. Benito had laughed, his big, brown eyes lit up from amusement while informing her he shied away because he knew one day she'd inherit the business and he didn't want to be in love with his future boss.

That conversation pushed her to solve the problem by going straight to her father and telling him she had no interest in taking over the business and handed heirship over to Benito.

Less than a month later, her father was murdered by Eduardo Juarez, a lower-level urchin responsible for making deliveries. Maria woke up to the sounds of screaming coming from the east wing. Even from her bedroom, she knew the agonizing wails were from her father. She ran to help, yelling for anyone to assist her, and upon opening the door to her father's bedroom, found Eduardo standing over the bloody mess that had once been the mighty Mario Alvarado. Dazed and still clutching the knife in his hand, the bastard fainted when she started screaming.

The yearning to feel Benito's lips devour her own happened less than two weeks later. She wasn't stupid and sensed he really didn't love her the way she loved him, but during the first month after losing her father, desperate for someone to offer solace and warmth, she convinced herself she was wrong.

She wasn't.

Their sexual relationship turned more sadistic and painful, and she could no longer ignore the truth—her fears were real—so she resigned herself to believe that giving up her body to only one man in exchange for continuing to live the life she was accustomed to was much better than becoming a used-up whore on the streets of San Salvador. The thought of servicing nameless men full of God-only-knows what type of diseases or their sick fantasies made her cringe in disgust.

When alone in her room, she hatched a plan while praying each night to the Virgin Mary. The request was simple and always the same—she wanted to become pregnant soon after marriage and give birth to a boy. That way, her father's bloodline and land holdings would continue on for generations. She was the last hope since Teresa was unable to bear children.

Wiping a straggler tear from her eye, unwilling to reminisce on tragedies of the past, she concentrates on her sister's upcoming nuptials. Since her measurements had drastically changed, the first item on their agenda was a meeting with the seamstress so the maid of honor dress could be altered to fit her new curves. She thinks the dress is a hideous color and design, yet the low neckline will accentuate her cleavage.

Everything will be perfect if her stomach stops rumbling. She'd asked the stewardess for water so many times during the flight she'd lost count, confused as to why her guts rolled and why she was so damned thirsty. Thirst gave way to hunger during the last ten minutes. She is ravenous, and for some strange reason, craves meat. Raw meat. Gobs and gobs of it. She nearly laughs out loud at the thought of shoveling the nastiness into her mouth because she's been a vegetarian ever since she was fifteen. Earlier, when she tried to eat a fresh carrot she'd brought with her, she nearly puked.

She's on her period, so she can't be pregnant. Looking around the cabin, she wonders if she encountered someone who had the flu or a cold. Everyone looks healthy, so maybe someone at the airport in San Salvador had been ill. Considering the city is a cesspool of filth and people, it is the most likely place she'd picked up a bug of some sort.

The pressure in the cabin changes as the airport comes into view. She reaches up and wipes her face, shocked by the heat radiating from her cheeks and forehead. She groans. A fever means she truly is coming down with something.

Brushing the annoying symptoms away, she stares at the beautiful diamond on her finger. Teresa will be so jealous when she sees the enormous rock in person. Twisting it so the light from the moon makes sparkles shimmer across the seatback, she thinks about Benito. They had a wicked argument before she left about his decision not to join her in Arizona. Business commitments, he'd told her when she pleaded earlier in the week. When she pushed the issue and continued begging, Benito yelled at her, which he never did, and stormed out of her bedroom.

The ugly conversation had been three days ago and not a word had been exchanged between them since. Benito didn't even come by her wing of the estate to say goodbye. Tears form in her eyes at the memory and slide down her hot cheeks. Brushing them away, she sets her jaw, forcing herself to concentrate her thoughts on visiting with Teresa.

After a jarring landing, the plane taxied up to the gate and came to a complete stop. She's in the first row of seats and the stewardess hands her the carryon bag, smiling and wishing her a pleasant stay in Phoenix.

Once through customs, she enters the main terminal and the anger regarding the situation with Benito disappears. Less than ten feet away stands a man dressed in a chauffer's uniform holding up a sign reading, "Maria Alvarado – Mi Cielo" in front of him. Her Benito loves her in his own way and made sure she is taken care of and arrives at

Teresa's in style. She smiles and waves to the nice-looking stranger, who immediately walks over and takes the bag from her shoulder.

"Ms. Alvarado, I'm Gregory, your driver for the evening. Your limo is waiting outside. Please, follow me."

A wave of dizziness makes her vision blur for a second. Fearing she may faint she reaches out a hand, grabbing the man's forearm. "How far? I'm afraid the flight left me feeling a bit off. Guess the excitement of my first experience in the air made me a little woozy."

"Do you need to sit down? Maybe I should get you a wheelchair?"

"No, I'll be fine if you'll just let me hang on to you while we walk. Okay?"

Gregory nods and Maria clings to his arm while they exit the terminal. Once they reach the doors leading to the parking area, she is soaked in sweat and burning pain radiates from her chest, extending to her head, legs, and arms. Her thighs are heavy and arms clunky and useless. She doesn't even have a chance to admire the black limo idling at the curb. By the time they reach it, she turns and throws up all over the sidewalk.

"Here, ma'am, have a seat. There's water in the small fridge to your left. I'll get you to your destination quickly."

Unable to do anything except nod in agreement, she tumbles into the cool leather, body splaying out across the entire back seat. She fumbles with her purse, trying to get to the cell to call Teresa. The bag slips off the slick seat and lands on the floorboard out of reach. She hears the driver close the door, shutting out the murmurs of grossed-out travelers who witnessed her vomit.

She tries one more time to grab the purse but stops short as the pain intensifies. She is having trouble breathing; her chest feels tight and heavy, like someone is sitting on it. Panic wells inside her at the realization she is thousands of miles from home and is at the mercy of a stranger.

The driver starts the car, and she senses the vehicle move as he guides it away from the curb. Grabbing on to the edge of the seat, she tries to sit up, yet another wave of dizziness makes the task impossible.

"Please, I think I need a doctor. Take me to the closest hospital? I can't seem to breathe."

"Not a problem, ma'am. That's exactly what I'm doing."

The tone in the man's voice is cold, eerie. All wrong. Fear spreads throughout her chest at the same time her limbs convulse.

Then, everything goes black.

***

"It sure is a shame to let such a hot piece go to waste. I should've sampled some of her before you slit her throat. Then again, she's been dead less than an hour, so she might still be warm enough to enjoy. Maybe I'll just pretend she's unconscious."

"That's disgusting, Santos. I'm going to pretend I didn't hear that."

"Give me a break, Carlos. You've done worse. Fucked worse. I still don't know if the last one in Vegas was male or female. Do you?"

Carlos Riviera snorts while wiping his bloodied fingers on a towel. He glances at the metal doors across the room, wondering when Gregory will return to help them clean up and stash the corpse.

Santos continues, "If I'd been the one picking a sacrificial mule to fill up with coke, I'da made sure she was so ugly her death would be a blessing on mankind."

Carlos ignores the blabbering of his brother. They had lots to do—and fast—so they can get back to Roberto's bachelor party before anyone notices they are missing. "There are plenty of others to fill the empty spot in Benito's bed, I'm sure. Looks aren't everything, Santos. See her fancy clothes and jewelry? I guarantee you she was a demanding bitch. She probably got mouthy with Benito. Then again, she was sick when Gregory brought her in. Maybe Benito didn't want to take care of an ailing woman, so he found himself a new, healthier toy. Now, quit talking and finish up. We still must dispose of her body."

Santos pushes back the fold of skin under the whore's right breast, exposing the implant. The other one sits on a metal tray behind him. He tugs on it twice before it pops out. "Oh, shit. This one has a hole! Damn, half the product leaked out. Huh—guess she wasn't sick after all. Just really fucked up. Oh, the irony. The great Mario Alvarado's daughter dies from an accidental overdose. Fucking classic."

Carlos runs over to the other side of the concrete slab serving as the operating table. Roberto owns the empty warehouse they use as a makeshift drug den and kill room for those who dare cross him. The place had once been a slaughterhouse, complete with numerous slabs in the middle for slicing up meat. The sloped floor gives way to an old drainage area, which makes clean up a breeze when Santos and Carlos are given such a task.

With no electricity, the area is hot as hell. The numerous candles lit around the table give them enough light to kill by but added to the heat. Sweat trickles down his nose and drips onto the dirty floor. Ignoring the bloody, cold body of the dead whore, he peers at the large bubble of silicon and then over to its mate on the tray.

"Stop staring and set it down before you waste anymore. Great, just fucking great! Benito and Roberto will think we shorted them. This screw up is your fault. You probably nicked it when cutting the bitch open while ogling her tits. I told you to be careful and make each cut with care!"

The men lapse into a heated argument about what to do and how to explain to Roberto and Benito what had happened to the cocaine. Neither man looks at the dead girl resting less than two feet away.

Santos hears the weird noise first. It is a strange gurgling sound, reminding him of when his cat, Escobar, is throwing up a hairball. Movement in his peripheral vision catches his attention, but not in enough time to warn Carlos.

Mute from horror, Santos cannot get his mouth to form words at the disturbing, impossible sight. The slippery implant falls from his trembling fingers, exploding upon impact with the floor. The liquid inside disappears down the grate in the floor. The formerly dead bitch jerks upright and lunges. Thick, purplish-red blood spills from the large gashes on her chest and neck. The mottled skin around the gaping wounds flaps in time with her quick movements. Grabbing Carlos from behind, she yanks his torso on top of her and sinks her teeth into his cheek.

Carlos and Santos scream at the exact same time.

"Help me, Santos! Get this bitch off me!"

Santos is frozen in place by paralyzing fear. He cannot stop staring, mind refusing to grasp the unbelievable situation. The thing in front of him continues to tear chunks of flesh from his brother's body, oblivious to the blows Carlos lands on her torso. They tumble off the slab onto the floor right next to his foot. The creature is fast and uses the opportunity to rip into Carlos' belly. Bright, red blood bursts from the wound. His brother shrieks in agony.

Adrenaline kicks in and the will to fight overrides the terror thumping inside his chest. He snatches the scalpel Carlos used less than an hour prior on the bitch, burying it into her back, pulls it loose, and stabs again.

Carlos' scream ceases after being disemboweled. Santos chokes back tears at the horrible sight of his brother ripped to shreds. The thing that killed him grumbles again, turning her attention to him. Blood covers every inch of her face. Strips of his brother's guts dangle from her mouth. Crouching, her black, dead eyes focus on Santos, she spins around and nips at his foot, gurgling and growling like a demon from Hell.

He scrambles backward but loses his footing on the slick floor, falling onto the tray table. The bowl holding the other implant crashes to the floor, followed by a strange popping sound. The scalpel clatters across the concrete after his hands shoot out to catch himself. The blade bounces away out of reach.

The drooling, snarling thing comes at him. He kicks his feet, landing a solid hit to her cheek, forcing the head to twist at an awkward angle. He hears bones crack from the impact, yet the blow doesn't seem to faze the creature. Her right hand catches his other foot, and though he tries to gain traction on the wet floor and move away, it is no use. Clamping her wet mouth around his calf muscle, he screams as she tears off nearly all the muscle in his lower leg.

Footsteps behind him allowed him to find his voice, "Help me! Jesus, kill it!"

He hears the gunshot at the same time the bitch's head explodes in front of him. The wet, sticky gore splashes across his face and body. The top of her head is gone, her mouth frozen wide yet somehow still holding the skin and muscle from his leg.

"What the fuck happened?" Gregory asks, his face pale and voice cracking.

Out of breath and heart pounding, Santos shakes his head. "Not a fucking clue. The drugs...they leaked into her...so all I can think of is they fried her brain or something. Just...help me, please? I've got to stop the bleeding."

Gregory leans down and grabs Santos, hefting him upright. After depositing him onto the closest slab, he mutters, "Take care of your leg. Stop the bleeding so there's less for me to clean up. We've gotta move fast in case someone overheard the gunshot. No time to waste. Where's the cleaver?"

Santos tries to remain stoic but fails. He leans over and throws up so hard he fears his eyeballs will burst. Once finished, he yanks off his shirt and wraps his leg. "In the bag next to Carlos. There's two, so help me get my leg wrapped because I want to be the one to chop that bitch up."

Gregory nods, moving across the floor to the bag. Over his shoulder, he says, "Looks like all the coke is wasted. Shit, Roberto said Benito told him this shipment was a new, special blend. Wonder what in the hell he put in there?"

Santos's stomach lurches again while staring at what is left of Carlos. A fleeting image of his mother wailing in grief flashes inside his mind. He dreads breaking the news. Fearing he will puke again he concentrates on his leg. The wound is bad and there is no way he can walk on his own. Burning pain shoots all the way into his chest. Gregory returns, sets the cleavers down, and helps secure his leg.

Just as Gregory tightens the makeshift tourniquet, the strange gurgling sound from before is back. Santos doesn't have time to say a word. Pushing Gregory out of the way, he throws himself across the slab and grabs a cleaver, ready to defend himself from the bloodied corpse of what used to be Carlos Juan Riviera.

He is too late.

What had formally been his baby brother descends on them. Internal organs hanging out, eyes black as coal, it attacks. The thing falls on top of Gregory, clawing, ripping, and biting through the man's exposed back. The shrieks of agony and terror mix with the gurgling. His head spins.

Santos only has one chance to bring the heavy cleaver down. The thick blade slices through tendons and muscle, stopping when it embeds in the spinal column. He lacks the strength to break the bone and the cleaver refuses to budge. The blow doesn't slow down the vicious attack. In fact, it gives his brother something else to concentrate on.

Santos.

Unable to run, he jumps off the slab and tries to hobble away on one leg. He makes it less than five feet before Carlos lands on his back.

Minutes later, the screaming stops. The only sound inside the warehouse comes from teeth grinding on flesh and bone.

Chapter 8 – Bad Batch

Friday, December 19th – 1:00 a.m.

BENITO SITS ON THE TILED, red roof the resort condo he owns in Colonia Escalon, watching the teeming nightlife of San Salvador through binoculars. Almost three hours have passed since he unleashed his men on the streets, so he is eager to watch the reactions of users. On the cusp of making his name famous throughout the world—at least in the circles of others like him—his legs shake from excitement and anticipation.

All the hard work and tension-filled moments of the last year are over. The scientists used the base material brought back from the botched incident in Laredo, creating the opposite of what the other fools originally intended. He'd been furious when his men returned without Dr. Berning and his little inside bug, Daryl Riverside, had been killed. The only reason he didn't take their lives is they handed him the bag containing vials and all the information needed on a flash drive to recreate Dr. Berning's work.

The idea was simple: If the chemical formula discovered by the American fools cured addiction, then one to increase the potency and need for more could be made from it as well by reversing the process. That was how Mario Alvarado looked at the idea, and Benito concurred, though he added his own personal touch. Originally, Mario only wanted to be informed of the progress, thinking the discovery would never materialize. If it did, his plan was to simply kill all those involved in the experiment, but Benito had other ideas.

After months of failures, the scientists made a breakthrough. The idea may have seemed simple, yet implementing it proved to be quite arduous for all involved in the process.

The scientists working to achieve the lofty agenda used all sorts of medical terminology that meant nothing to him when explaining their accomplishment. All he cared about was the bottom line—did they complete his plan to ensure those who ingested any sort of narcotic become irrevocably addicted because if successful, there would never be a shortage of clientele.

Ever.

Seven months later, the scientists under his care succeeded, so he put the next phase of his plan into motion and sold the formula to over one-hundred cartels around the world for a very hefty sum, each agreeing to deploy the serum at the same time in upcoming shipments across the globe. Drug lords in China, Russia, Afghanistan, Columbia, Brazil, Australia, and even Germany were buyers. As an extra touch, he decided to terminate the annoying relationship with Maria at the same time. He wanted to get a batch to Roberto quickly, so he had his private surgeon use liquid cocaine rather than silicone to pump up her boobs. He made sure Maria wouldn't get the chance to attend Teresa's wedding, and that the drugs would slip through customs undetected.

The last two days he spent holed up inside the penthouse floor of the condo, going over all the instructions with his team. His personal pilot, Fernando, even flew him deep into the jungle so Benito could oversea the manufacturing process. When he poured the concoction into a large vat of freshly made cocaine, the feeling was close to orgasmic.

Now, fifty of his lieutenants hit the packed bars and clubs of Ciudad Merliot, pockets full of the new batch of coke. Another fifty spread out through the shanty towns along the city's fringes. He didn't trust the operation to his hundreds of foot soldiers because they are simpletons, unable to grasp the magnitude of his ingenious plans. He concluded the best course of action was to hook the rich and the poor at the same time, and to ensure this worked and people took the bait, he told the men to give away hits for free. Between the hundred men, they would be distributing—free of charge—nearly three kilos of pure, uncut cocaine.

The plan does pose a financial risk up front, yet he's counting on the rewards in the future outweighing the losses in the present.

His cell phone vibrates and his heart rate spikes. He hopes it was a text from one of his men, not another pathetic, tear-filled communication from the other Alvarado whore, Teresa. During the last day-and-a-half, she's called him so many times he's lost count. At first, he took her calls and tried to act worried as well, assuring Teresa he would do whatever necessary to locate the missing Maria. After the tenth call, he'd lost his temper and shut the whiny bitch down, promising to take the next flight to Phoenix to assist in the search.

Extracting the phone from his pocket, he smiles. The call was from Roberto's private number used only for communication with Benito. Figuring he is calling to report on the results of the experiment in Phoenix, he touches the screen.

Before he can finish a sentence, Roberto interrupts, voice strained and sirens wailing in the background. "Don't deploy! Don't deploy! Something's wrong!"

Benito's mouth goes dry. Heavy static makes hearing Roberto's words difficult. "Calm down and say again? I can't understand..."

"People...dying...coming...back...spreading...abort! For...sake...abort!"

The sound of Roberto's terrified voice is drowned out by screams rising from the city below. Disconnecting the call, Benito lifts the binoculars to his eyes. As he focuses the lenses, the smell of smoke wafts through the tropical night air. The screams are joined by numerous sirens from police cruisers and ambulances. Brightly colored lights flood the streets and alleyways. Throngs of people run through the crowded streets, trampling each other in a panicked effort to flee.

A sense of foreboding squashes the joy from seconds ago. His cell phone vibrates in quick succession, an indicator texts are flooding the screen. Lowering the binoculars as his stomach churns, he glances at the vibrant screen and sees sixteen texts and counting, all from separate numbers.

Stunned, he clicks on the newest one. "What have you done? This stuff is poison!"

Then another: "I'm going to hunt you down for this! Slice your fucking balls off!"

And another: "You said this would guarantee clients for life! Instead, they are dying in droves! AND COMING BACK!"

The screams from below are louder, drawing his attention away from the phone. The sickening feeling swirling inside his gut increases. He takes one last look at the streets, hoping to find the reason behind the chaos is from a gunman or wild animal, but he knows he won't.

Gunshots ring throughout the area in quick succession. Automatic weapons—he knows the sound. Zooming in on one spot, he follows a stream of citizens running down a small alleyway, hands shaking as he searches for what sent them into hysterics. A policeman dressed in full riot gear makes his way through the crowd, crouches, and trains his weapon behind them. Benito watches the flashes of light spray out the end as the cop fires off several rounds into a woman's body.

The bullets rip through the young woman's chest, thigh, and shoulder. She falls onto the brick street, landing at an odd, unnatural angle as the crowd scatters. The policeman stands, gun at the ready, and moves toward her, but only makes it three steps before she pushes herself up from the ground and jumps, toppling the cop over. Her right leg is bent backward, and left arm hangs limply at her side, yet she moves at an unbelievable pace.

In a flash, she is on top of the stunned cop. She tears his throat out with her teeth.

Benito doesn't have a chance to see anything else because the lights of San Salvador flicker once then go out.

Controlling his rising fear while securing his gear, he scrambles to leave the rooftop. Mindful of his steps on the slick terra cotta, he is only a few feet away from the door leading to the stairwell. Fumbling around in his pocket for the keycard to unlock the door, he curses under his breath while trying to extract it. The sounds coming from all around him rival a war zone. The gunfire and screams increase, joined now by three explosions strong enough the building shakes. He freezes, trying to maintain his balance, and for a split second, succeeds, but when the fourth explosion hits, he loses his footing and falls backward.

He catches himself and remains on the roof, but the keycard doesn't. If flies from his fingers and slides off the edge, disappearing into the night.

"Fuck!"

Trapped twenty stories in the air with the building closest to him over thirty feet away, panic threatens to overtake his mind. Even if he was on a flat surface and could get a running start, jumping such a far expanse is impossible. Glancing up to the sky, wincing at the bright, orange light from numerous fireballs across the city, he grabs the cell phone and dials Fernando's number. On the third ring, he answers. Benito hears the whirr of the helicopter blades and lets out a sigh of relief.

"You still on the rooftop, boss?"

"Only until you get here. ETA?"

"Three minutes, tops."

"Make it two."

Benito disconnects the call, ignoring the continuous notifications of new texts. He rises and searches the sky for Fernando, straining his ears for the sound of the helicopter yet hearing nothing except the sounds of San Salvador under siege.

Body coated in sweat and heart racing; the shakes set in. If something goes wrong with the chopper and Fernando doesn't rescue him, he won't survive.

The sound he's yearning to hear pulls him out of his own dance with hysteria. The chopper hovers about fifty feet above him. A rope ladder clanks as it hits the tiles of the roof ten feet to his right, followed by white light illuminating the entire building from the spotlight.

Afraid he might lose his footing from the downdraft of the blades, Benito sinks to all fours and crawls across the roof. When his fingers wrap around the rope ladder, he calls upon every quaking muscle in his body to pull himself up. The climb up the swaying rope is terrifying, but less so than the alternative of staying on the roof.

Once safely inside, he yanks the swaying ladder and stows it away, secures the headset, and gives the thumbs up to Fernando, who immediately banks the machine and soars through the dark skies.

"Sorry I'm late. I had to fight off some…thing…before I could refuel."

Still shaking, Benito nods. "Get us to the estate. Fast."

"Of course. From the sounds and sights up here, you'd think we're under attack or something. News mentioned an outbreak of some sort, which makes sense. The thing I ran into at the airport seemed sick."

Benito hears the fear in Fernando's voice and glances over at him. A large bandage covers his forearm, blood seeping through the layers. "What happened?"

"The guy—or thing—at the airport bit me. Can you believe that shit? I had to shoot him right there on the runway. Once in the air, I tried to listen further to what was going on but then the radio went silent. It's eerie. Not even the police channels are active. There's nothing but static. Any idea what's going on?"

Benito stares across the expanse of the dark city below, the only lights from emergency personnel and countless fires. A strange feeling settles over him as the gravity of the situation hits home.

His scientists did this—and judging by the communications from others—the nightmare is happening across the globe. He wonders if the sabotage was done on purpose by the scientists. Maybe it was their way of paying him back for forcing them to work, knowing if they failed, Benito would make good on his threats to kill their families? No, they wouldn't dare. They simply miscalculated the correct chemical formulation.

A memory from months ago roars to the forefront of his thoughts. The results of the formula on mice worked perfectly. Benito was insistent on implementing his plan during the holiday season, which is the busiest time of year. Instead of listening to the scientists, he decided not to test the formula on humans. His colossal mistake of relying on data collected from mice in the lab has come back to haunt him.

Whatever the reason for the enormous mistake, once he finds them, Benito will interrogate them until they cannot speak another word and then slaughter them like cattle.

Though not a believer in any sort of organized religion, he says a silent prayer before answering Fernando. "When the end of the world happens, does it really matter why?"

Chapter 9 - Collapse

Saturday December 20th – 6:00 a.m.

"REGINA? YOU DECENT?"

Sensing the odd tone in Reed's voice, worried it may have something to do with Jesse, Regina takes a deep breath. "Just lacing up my boots. Come on in."

Reed opens the bedroom door and scoots inside, shutting it behind him. His face is pale; jaw clenched tight. Her gaze falls to his waist. Reed wears his Sam Brown belt, and a loaded nine mil sits in the holster.

She swallows the sense of nagging worry. "What's wrong? You look like shit. And you're armed. If you are going deer hunting with that, you'd do better with a rifle."

"Obviously, you haven't watched or listened to any news this morning."

"Uh, no. I've been up a total of ten minutes, which included my shower."

Reed walks across the room and joins Regina on the bed, setting her cell phone between them. "No time for your twisted sense of humor, sis. The station has called numerous times, so I figured something was up and called while you were in the shower. Geenie said there's a big pileup on I-30 involving an 18-wheeler and several vehicles. Multiple casualties."

"Damn, I hate those big rigs! God, I hope no kids are involved."

"Hush, Regina. The accident isn't why I came in here."

The worry from seconds ago morphs into fear and spreads across her chest. She nods for him to continue.

"News reports are flooding in from all over the world. There's something going on—not just here but everywhere—and no one can give a plausible answer as to what's behind it."

"Behind what, Reed?"

"Power outages, fires, explosions, riots, and people walking around who shouldn't be."

She slugs him in the shoulder hard enough to make her fist hurt before snatching the phone, shocked to see she's missed seven calls and has numerous text messages. "You're the one with a twisted sense of humor. If that little joke is your way to helping me deal with all the carnage from a semi accident, I don't find it funny."

"Shut up, Regina!" Reed grabs her wrist with such force her initial instinct is to punch him in the face. "You need to see what I mean. Words simply won't suffice."

Crossing the room, Reed flicks on the small TV and turns the volume down while glancing at the door. She is furious he still wants to play the stupid game. She opens her mouth to tear him a new one, but what she sees on the screen traps the words in her throat.

The jerky image is from a cell phone video. A passenger in a car with an arm sticking out the window is filming an accident on the freeway. Mangled, twisted metal is strewn across several lanes, glass and debris spread even further. Tendrils of smoke rise from demolished vehicles. The blacktop is coated in gas and blood.

Though disturbing, those images aren't what caught her attention.

A man crouching over and shoveling the innards of a dead female EMT into his mouth is what's rendered her mute.

Another EMT comes into view and tries distracting the man. When he looks up, the face is covered in blood and gore. A large piece of metal protrudes through the neck and another, bigger one, pierces the chest cavity. The video zooms in, and she notices his eyes are solid black.

And his neck is broken.

Gasping, she covers her mouth with both hands.

The other EMT has a stun gun and gets close enough to strike, but the man with the mortal injuries jumps over the corpse he's been munching on like a hurdler in the Olympics. Latching his broken, bloodied fingers around the EMT's arm holding the weapon, his head juts forward, sinking his teeth deep into the man's neck. Blood spurts out, coating them, and the ground, in seconds.

Unwilling to look anymore, Regina lets her gaze fall to the ticker at the bottom of the screen. It reads, "Phoenix motorist captures video of injured man attacking rescuers on Interstate 10...Arizona Governor deploys National Guard...All travel, including air and vehicle, has been halted in Arizona...Stay tuned for similar videos from New York, Seattle, Los Angeles, Afghanistan and China...President Thompson to address the nation at..."

Shaking, she grabs her belt and jacket, motioning for Reed to turn off the television. "Stay here with Jesse. Don't let her leave your side! She's to stay home from work today. I've got to go."

"I know. I promise to take care of her. You just take care of the citizens—and yourself."

"Thank you. Keep your cell always charged and with you. Oh, and please, don't let Jesse watch—"

"I won't let her near anything electronic. She doesn't need to see any of this. Go."

Adrenaline in overdrive, she spins on her heels and races through the house. Once inside the cruiser, she fires it up and secures the wireless headset, unwilling to risk using the radio, fully aware locals are monitoring communications. Using voice commands, she calls the station while backing out of the driveway.

"It's about damn time, Chief! Things are crazy here," Geenie yells.

"I understand there's an accident on 30? Which mile marker?"

"Ninety-eight. Right at the start of the construction. State boys are already there. Roger and Clint are helping with traffic control."

Regina flicks on the lights without the siren and heads into town. "I'll let them handle it. On my way. Should be there in less than two minutes."

Geenie clears her throat and Regina hears a hitch in her voice. She can tell Geenie is fighting back tears. "Good. Because you just received an email marked urgent from the Governor."

Regina blows through a stoplight; grateful no one is on the road. "What does it say?"

"I can't open it. Oh, another just arrived. Says a code will be sent to you."

Regina's phone beeps with an incoming text. The number is blocked, and the message simply contains a long string of numbers. "To my phone. Yeah, just got it."

"What's going on, Chief? You know, I don't put too much stock in what I see or hear on the news because most of it is crap. But what I saw earlier was like watching a horror movie!"

Regina pulls into the parking lot, tires barking as she tromps on the brakes. Yanking off the headset, she exits the car, preferring to answer Geenie in person.

The elderly woman's face is pale, eyes the size of saucers. "Calm down, my friend. Let me see what the Governor sent and then we'll sort through all this mess. If something bad is happening, we need to stay strong. Residents will panic. They'll need someone with a cool head to keep things together. Okay?"

Geenie stands and moves so Regina can sit. "Okay."

"Go get some coffee or water. Stretch your legs and take a breather."

Without a word, Geenie turns and heads to the kitchen. Regina waits until she hears the rattle of cups before opening the email. She enters the password and waits. In seconds, another box opens. She leans closer to read the screen.

"The National Guard has been deployed. As of 6:05 a.m., I implemented the Arkansas Emergency

Operations Plan. AR EOP is designed to reduce vulnerability and loss of life and damage to property during any form of disaster or crisis.

We are working in conjunction with the federal authorities. Our goal is to rapidly respond and assess the current nationwide catastrophe. The situation is a large-scale event, requiring all levels of government to take proactive response measures.

I have directed all members of the Highway Patrol to secure all roads coming in to and out of our state. No residents will be allowed to leave until all citizens are accounted for and tested. Representatives from the state health department will arrive in each county's seat in less than an hour. All local and county law enforcement agencies are to instruct every citizen in their respective jurisdiction to report to the local high school, which will serve as the Joint Field Office until containment is reached.

Once a citizen is tested and deemed clear, they may return home, but must remain in their local area until all seventy-five counties have completed the testing. Residents who test positive must be immediately quarantined.

The National Guard will take charge of each county jail. Citizens who test positive will be quarantined in jail. Biohazard suits are to be worn during the entire operation."

Regina re-reads the entire statement twice. The words on the screen send waves of fear throughout her body and for a split second, she wonders if she's experiencing a nightmare. She whispers to the silent screen, "Dear God, what the hell is going on?"

Geenie is coming down the hall, so Regina hits the print button before closing the email, deleting it as instructed. Fingers shaking, she picks up the pages off the printer, shoves them into her jacket pocket, and stands.

"So what did...oh, shit. You look like a ghost just passed through you. Are we under attack from another demented group from overseas? Did someone hit us with a dirty bomb or bio attack?"

Forcing her voice to remain calm, Regina motions for Geenie to sit. "Listen to me. You are going to be very busy in the next few minutes. Swamped. AR EOP has been enacted. Get Roger and Clint on the radio and tell them to return to the station immediately. I need their help getting everyone over to the high school. EBS will activate in five minutes, instructing everyone to go there. People are going to flip and start calling to ask why. Do not try and answer their questions, just repeat the edict to go to the school. Got it?"

Geenie's bottom lip trembles. "What if they want to talk to you, ask you what's going on?"

She heads down the hall to the closet housing extra weapons. "Just reiterate they need to go to the high school. They'll be safe there. If someone pressures you for more, hang up."

Before Geenie can respond, the phone rings. Though a seasoned, twenty-year dispatcher, Geenie hesitates. Regina watches the distraught woman close her eyes and mumble something under her breath before reaching and grabbing the receiver. "9-1-1. What's your emergency?"

Unlocking the closet, Regina yanks a shotgun from the rack and loads it with shells. Inside the small space, she whispers, "God, help us."

She jumps when her cell phone vibrates. Looking down to see who is calling, a cold shiver races up her spine. "I don't need to ask you why you're calling. You got the same email."

Sheriff Roger Calhoun clears his throat. The sound of radio chatter in the background makes the hairs stand up on Regina's neck. "Yep. Some nerdy looking fools dressed like they're ready to walk on the moon just arrived, along with armed military escorts. They just waltzed in here and took over my jail. Bastards had the nerve to tell me and my deputies to leave. Jim Grayson demanded to know what was going on and get this: one of the soldiers handcuffed him and went to lock him up!"

She forces herself not to sound frightened at the tone in the sheriff's voice. "Went to lock him up? What, did the soldier change his mind?"

"No. The guy in the drunk tank did."

"Sheriff, just spit out what you're trying to say. Time's wasting."

"You know Ricky Baber, right?"

"Doesn't every law official in this county? Biggest crack head around, and I'm pretty sure the one who got Jesse hooked on meth. Why?"

"We picked him up last night after he rolled his truck. He didn't seem to have any injuries, but guess we were wrong."

"What happened?"

"Jim Grayson and his armed escort found Ricky face down in the cell. When they went in to check on him, he jumped up off the floor and attacked Jim and the soldier. Ricky tore Jim's lips and nose off before the grunt shot him in the head. It was utter chaos!"

"Holy shit!"

"We tried to take Jim to the hospital, but the guys in white took him away and refused to tell us where they were taking him, or why. When I tried to intervene, one of the bastards stuck a rifle in my face."

A sense of dread crawls through her mind. "Let's finish this discussion once we get everybody to the school, okay? Ears might be listening."

"Agreed. See you there. Oh, and Parker?"

"Yes?"

"Stay safe."

"You, too, Sheriff."

Regina disconnects the call, mind spinning from the news. Part of her feels a twinge of satisfaction, a sense of justice, knowing Ricky Baber is dead. The other part wonders if he is like the disgusting thing she'd seen on the news earlier. Dead yet moving. Still in the dark as to what is really going on, the terror of the situation threatens to overtake common sense. Forcing it deep down inside, she pulls herself together because now was not the time to freak out. Her family, friends, neighbors, and even strangers in Rockport, need her to remain calm.

She finally manages to finish loading three guns when Roger's terrified voice crackles from the mic on her shoulder. "Need backup. Shots fired. Officers down. Repeat, officers down. Bullets aren't stopping them...oh, my God!"

Without thinking or saying a word to Geenie, Regina grabs a shotgun and bursts out the front door.

***

"Good morning, sunshine. I love you. I'll be back shortly. Duty calls."

President Arthur Thompson kisses Melissa's warm forehead. She stares at him, eyes still heavy from sleep, nods once, and then rolls over, burying her head underneath the thick comforter.

His footsteps are quick and loud while exiting the bedroom. Early mornings and late evenings are when he usually appears—briefly—and pretends to care about his daughter. The morning ritual is always the same. He brings in fresh flowers, sets them in the vase on the desk, kisses her forehead, and then makes false promises to come back soon. Enduring the same bullshit for almost eight years made her immune to the hollow words.

Her friends at school all envy her position as the daughter of the world's most powerful man, but she hates it. When her mother was still alive, living under constant scrutiny and ever-present guards had been tolerable, but after her mom died, things went downhill to the point Melissa wished she could just disappear.

She craves a normal life to make stupid, teenage mistakes without fearing how every move she makes will be scrutinized and picked apart by the media. How fantastic would it be to cut her hair and wear a style of clothing meant for a fifteen-year-old, not a Catholic schoolgirl from 1950, or to get drunk one night with her friends and pierce her ears.

Have an actual relationship with a guy.

The last two dudes who made her panties wet felt the same way she did. She knew it. Felt it. Saw it behind their eyes when they stared at her in class. She is aware she isn't gorgeous, but her jet-black hair, blue eyes, and curves, compliments of her mother, all combined into a nice package, but that didn't seem to matter to Stephan Cumberland and Matthew Guss. They kept their hands far away from Melissa's body. With all the tight security constantly hovering around, and who her father is, dashed any hopes of Melissa getting kissed, felt up, or fucked.

She cannot wait for January. The second term of well-loved and respected President Thompson will be over, and the duties passed on to the obnoxious blowhard, President-Elect Ronald Krump. Melissa Renee Thompson will finally be released from the prison others around the globe called the White House, and the freaking slew of goons who guard her will be hewn down to only one.

Fully awake, she groans inwardly. Stephanie Roseburg, known to the staff as Melissa's caretaker, is breathing heavy. The middle-aged Secret Service agent is a gruff, harsh woman who rarely cracks a smile. Melissa hates to even look at her. The woman isn't exactly ugly in the features department, but the ugliness inside her soul trumps the bland face.

For the first six years she'd been assigned to guard Melissa, the woman rarely spoke. She nicknamed her Sourpuss Stephanie, a term she only uses when around friends. After the death of her mother, the old bitch attempted to show some emotion, but it was flat and obviously fake.

She despises the woman and was thankful when her father informed her Agent Roseburg would not be the one assigned to watch over her after they left the White House. She'd been so excited she went back to her room on the second floor and jumped up and down on the bed so hard the frame broke.

While still underneath the covers, it dawns on her that the woman's respirations are different than normal. Plus, her father's voice seemed off. Normally, his usual morning greeting is spoken in a halting monotone, like even he knows the words are premeditated and calculated. A recorded message on auto play. The last time he sounded sincere and full of real emotion was the morning her mother died.

Poking her head out from under the comforter, she notices the flower vase is empty, which is odd She looks over at Stephanie. The woman wasn't looking in her direction because all her attention is focused on the tablet resting on her lap, ear buds firmly stuck in place. The rosy tinge usually in her plump cheeks is gone. She looks worried, the lines on her brow knit together while staring at the screen.

"Stephanie, what's wrong?"

No answer.

Climbing out of bed, she reaches for the small purse on the dresser before walking over to where the agent sits, trying to see what Stephanie is watching. Startled by her presence, the woman clicks a button, and the screen goes black before Melissa has a chance to see anything. Stephanie removes the earbuds.

"I asked you what's going on. What were you watching?"

"Nothing that concerns you, Miss Thompson. Ready for breakfast?"

She can tell the woman was lying. A tremor of worry makes the skin above her right eye twitch. "No, I'm not hungry. I want to know what's going on. Why is dad acting so strange, and why do you look like you're about to pass out?"

Rising from the chair, Stephanie deposits the tablet in the black satchel on the table. "It is not for me to discuss such matters with you, Miss Thompson. Your father will brief you after he delivers his speech to the nation. Why don't you take a nice, relaxing bath? It will help your cramps."

Annoyed by the dismissal of her worries and the fact the old bitch knows she's on the rag, Melissa huffs and storms into the bathroom. "Since you already know I'm bleeding, I suppose you won't be shocked when I ask you to get me some more tampons, right?"

Without saying a word, the agent nods and exits the bedroom.

Melissa slams the door, locks it, turns on the faucet, and settles down on the toilet seat. She opens the small bag and removes a single tampon, a gift from her best friend, Monique. Nestled inside the plastic wrapper is a tampon alright, one passed underneath the stall at school the day before, but what makes this blood cork special is instead of being a wad of cotton, it is hollowed out and inside is a baggie full of enough white powder to make living under the probing eyes of the nation tolerable.

Opening the baggie, she dumps out the cocaine onto the countertop. Knowing Stephanie will return at any minute—and probably has a key to the bathroom—she wastes no time. Bending down, she snorts the small pile up. The familiar burn makes her smile as she balls up the plastic and swallows it.

The bathtub is full, so she slides inside the warm water, surprised at how quickly the rush happened. She stifles a giggle. Monique told her yesterday while in the girl's bathroom swapping tampons, the stuff came straight from Columbia. Monique's older sister's boyfriend is the son of a Columbian dignitary and had just returned from an early Christmas celebration in Bogota.

While pretending to fix Melissa's ponytail in the bathroom, Monique had whispered, "This will make your Christmas merry, I promise. Carrie said Ricardo mentioned it was hard-core stuff. He brought back enough for the big party tonight at the Columbian consulate in New York. Oh, the holidays! Deck the nose with toots of candy, fa-la-la-la la!"

Monique wasn't kidding. The stuff is unbelievable—the best she's ever snorted. For the next few minutes, Melissa lets the frothy, fragrant water and the extreme high control her thoughts, rather than wondering what catastrophe in the world her father is working on fixing.

Minutes later, as she hears Stephanie knock on the door, announcing her feminine products are on the nightstand, she changes her mind about breakfast. "Stephanie?"

"Yes, Miss Thompson?"

"Please order me some bacon, sausage, and a side of oatmeal. Um, on second thought, scratch the oatmeal. Oh, and make sure to tell the cook I want the meat rare. And water. Several bottles of ice water. I'm thirsty. Must be from losing so much blood."

"Of course."

She closes her eyes and wonders what kind of new shit is mixed in with the coke. Though she's only been a user since her mom died, she normally doesn't have an appetite when high. Lack of hunger is another perk of the white stuff and helped her drop eight pounds of baby fat.

Pushing the thought aside, she finishes washing and stands and picks up a towel. A twinge of pain inside her chest makes her wince. Assuming she pulled something at volleyball practice the day before, she ignores it and continues drying off.

Grabbing her favorite lotion from the counter, she squirts out a handful and bends down to coat her legs, but a wave of dizziness makes the room spin and stars appear. Reaching out her hands to the counter to steady herself, they slip off the slick marble and she loses her balance, tumbles to the floor, smacking her head on the edge of the counter on the way. "Ouch!"

Stephanie's at the door, calling her name, asking if she is okay. The voice sounds distant and muffled. The most intense pain she'd ever experienced pounds throughout her chest, taking her breath away. The intense burning makes her forget all about the headache. She tries to speak but cannot get her lips to move.

Crawling on all fours, she reaches the door handle at the same time vomit spews from her mouth.

The last thing she remembers is unlocking the door and Stephanie rushing to her side, screaming into the walkie-talkie for help.

And how damned good her blood, as well as the agent's, smells.

Chapter 10 - On Target

Saturday December 20th – 6:30 a.m.

"YOU'RE SURE? All sources agree it's a real crunch?"

"Damn straight. This ain't no drill, Walt. Lamar is at his station and reported massive troop movement coming this way. EBS just came on, telling us all to go to the high school. Time to switch to the CB from here on out. This is a C.C. event my friend."

Walter Addison snorts into the phone so hard he nearly drops it. He hears the excitement and worry in Curt Campbell's voice. "If that's true, ain't no way I'm following some stupid directive like that! Be all bunched up like sheep at a slaughterhouse? No way. I ain't letting my family be under the control of the government any more than what they already are."

"I'm right there with you, Walt. We knew this day would come, but you know what? Part of me hoped I was just a paranoid old fool."

Walter stands and trots to the front door, locking it as he stares out the picture window into the empty streets. "Me, too. Stay safe, Curt. We're ready for whatever they throw at us."

"Amen, brother. Amen."

Disconnecting from the call, Walt heads back into the kitchen. His wife of twenty-seven years, Martha, is still fixing breakfast, oblivious to what is going on. Pausing in the doorway, he watches her cook. Her light blonde hair with streaks of gray is pulled back into a ponytail, and the lovely locks cascade down to the middle of her slender back. The years had been kind to her for Martha is just as beautiful as when they met in high school.

His wife stood by him through numerous deployments overseas and all the nightmares he'd endured upon returning home. She even put up with his rants about the government and decision to become a prepper. The first few years into the new lifestyle, Martha didn't say much or voice her opinions on the subject, she just went along with his plans. However, after about three years in and studying up on things on her own, the look of doubt and misgiving disappeared from her face.

His thoughts while staring at the only woman he's ever loved are a weird mixture. Pride fills his heart because he knows they are ready yet fear pounds inside his mind at the knowledge they must be.

Taking a deep breath, he walks up behind her and kisses her neck. "Honey? Please sit. We need to talk. Where's Turner? He needs to hear this, too."

Martha hands him a cup of coffee. Her beautiful blue eyes make his heart skip a beat. "I think he's still in the shower. Were you talking to Curt?"

Motioning for her to join him at the kitchen table, he nods.

"What's going on?" Martha pulls out a chair.

"Let's wait until Turner…"

"Wait for me for what?"

Both turn their heads at the sound of Turner's voice from the doorway. Walt pulls out the chair next to him. "Sit. Family meeting. Code Crimson."

Martha's eyes widened; lips forming a small circle. "Code Crimson—not a drill?"

"No."

Turner remains frozen in the doorway, his wet hair sticking up in every direction, face freshly shaven. The terror behind his eyes makes him look like a little boy. His fingers shake while fiddling with his cell phone.

"Turn it off. Right now."

"Dad, I've got to warn Jesse!"

"Jesse is her mother's responsibility, not yours. Turn it off. You know the protocol for Code Crimson."

"Walt, stop yelling at him. You just officially freaked us both out. What exactly are we dealing with?"

"The type of biological used is unknown at this time. All I know for sure is we are to report to the high school."

Martha stifles a gasp. "Are we? Going to go to the school?"

He shakes his head. "No. Going to our beta location in ten minutes, tops. Lamar Wilson is on point out in the woods by I-30. Curt said he reported a large caravan of troops heading our way and ETA is about ten minutes. We've got to get out of here before they have a chance to start counting heads and realize we're gone."

"We sticking to the full plan for location beta?" Martha asks.

"Absolutely."

Walt sees the change in his beloved wife's face. Fear, anger, and determination turn her pretty features into stone. She stands and walks to the sink, dumping out her coffee.

"Turner—you know your duties." Straightening her shoulders, Martha's voice is low yet strong. "Make sure all electronics and anything linking us to the outside world are disconnected. I'll get our gear and masks while your dad attends to his tasks of securing the house."

Walter Addison—the fifty-eight-year-old machine shop owner, married to his high school sweetheart for almost three decades—has never been more in love with his wife than he is right now.

***

Mind spinning, Turner races into the living room and unplugs the big screen TV and then reaches behind it, disconnecting the cable from the wall. He's practiced the drill so many times, the muscle movement is ingrained. Though he'd never admit it out loud, he is grateful he is the son of two parents who'd prepared him to survive when things went to shit.

And they just did. A fucking face-plant into the bowels of hell.

For a few seconds after his father dropped the news onto their laps, Turner had been full of doubt. Those thoughts vanished when Seth sent him a battery of text messages, each containing links to videos online. After leaving the kitchen, his parents engaged in conversation, Turner paused in the hallway and clicked on the first link.

What appeared on the small screen of his cell phone made his skin crawl.

His father has been right all along.

He hears a strange noise outside, so he peeks out the window. His heart immediately thunders inside his chest when he sees armored vehicles crammed with troops in full gear rumbling through the street. He loses count after the first thirty.

"So much for Lamar's great skills Ten minutes my ass!"

Running to the stairs leading to the basement, he breaks one of the rules and calls Jesse. By the time he reaches the bottom of the stairs, he is in full panic mode because the call went straight to voicemail. "Shit!"

Shoving the phone into his pocket, he flicks on the overhead light, opens the small metal box housing the internet connection, and cuts the wires. Once finished, he stops and listens to the sounds from upstairs. He can tell both his parents are on the other side of the house, so he tries Jesse again.

Same results.

He shuts down all the thoughts vying for attention inside his mind and focuses on two: his parents and Jesse.

Deprived of her sweet presence for years, he'd spent countless nights worrying and praying for her safety while she was gone. He'd been miserable without her, and when she returned from rehab, sober and apologetic, begging for forgiveness from all the pain she put him—and others—through, he was thrilled. They resumed their relationship not long after, and he thanked the Lord every night for the transformation of the woman he loved.

He'd saved two hundred dollars from each paycheck for the last six months and bought the best engagement ring he could afford, planning to surprise her on Christmas Eve, presenting the ring while on one knee in front of the massive display of lights at the courthouse.

Considering Hot Spring County will soon be under control of the military, he decides to show Jesse how much he loves her in a different way.

It is time to put the skills his father hammered into his brain and body for years to use by staying at the side of the girl he refuses to live without. There is simply no way he will leave with his family and head to the cave near Blanchard Springs and leave Jesse behind.

Period.

Glancing up to the ceiling while listening to the sounds of his parents tromping around, he makes his choice. Even though he loves them, he knows they will be fine. No two people in Rockport are better prepared for what is coming than Walter and Martha Addison.

Jesse Parker isn't. It is his job to protect her.

Taking the stairs two at a time, he exits the basement and slips into his room, shuts the door, runs to the closet, puts his boots and jacket on, and then grabs his prep bag from the top shelf. After slinging the pack over his shoulder, he scrawls out a note to his parents, leaves it on the bed, dashes to the window, and climbs out. Dropping down to the ground below, he glances around the yard, sees the coast is clear, and bursts from his position, heading to the cover of trees behind the house.

As he runs, he hears the booming sound of a man's voice over a bullhorn. The deep voice shouts instructions to his neighbors to meet at the high school immediately.

"Like hell." Turner whispers into the quiet woods.

Pushing his muscles to their limits, he says a silent prayer, asking God to let him make it to Jesse's, and to keep her, and his family, safe from whatever is going on.

***

Jesse Parker rolls over and stares at the pink teddy bear next to her, smiling while recalling the day Turner won it for her at the county fair. The eight-inch stuffed animal cost him nearly ten dollars and provided a lot of laughter as he kept trying to shoot three yellow ducks in a row.

She hears her mother and uncle talking but cannot make out what they were saying. Figuring they are whispering about her, plotting their plan of action to keep an eye on her whereabouts twenty-four-seven, she ignores them. The need for coffee and a hot shower overrides the desire to eavesdrop on the conversation. Even though she loves them both, the continual worry about whether she will slip and start using drugs again drives her crazy.

Thinking about all the ugly, painful counseling sessions during and after her stint in rehab, she sighs. The counselor told her the overprotectiveness would happen and would probably take several years to fade away. Jesse had nodded, tears running down her cheeks, crushed that her stupid mistakes and choices caused deep scars inside the minds of those who loved her. Fighting off the feelings of guilt and remorse is a daily struggle.

Shivering at the chill in the air and the ever-present sense of shame, she shoves her feet into the fluffy pink slippers next to the bed, glances out the window, and guesses it is close to seven, which gives her plenty of time to get ready for her shift at ten.

After using the bathroom, she stares at her reflection in the mirror. It took her three full months after returning home to stop bursting into tears when looking at herself. Meth destroyed her features. Some of the damage was fixable, like her teeth. She'd lost six of them and had to endure weeks of dental procedures. Her hair had finally started to thicken again and turn shiny rather than hanging in a dull, shapeless mess against her head. She takes showers now without worrying clumps would fall out, which is a blessing.

However, there are some physical side effects she fears would never heal. One is the color of her skin. Though she's always had a fair complexion, before she became a hardcore addict, the pink undertone in her skin gave off a healthy glow, but that is gone now, replaced by a sallow tint.

The other side effect—the one that bothers her the most—is the sunken cheeks and thin body. According to the scale, she has gained fifteen pounds of healthy weight, yet her face and torso still look as though she is an active user. Ever since Thanksgiving, she had been stuffing herself with as many calories her stomach would allow, hoping to wipe away the remaining traces of her former life and stop seeing the wounded, worried look behind her mother's eyes.

She sneezes three times in a row; her sinuses throb in response and her eyes water. She's been blessed with her father's immune system. Her mother used to tease them, calling them human barometers, because both suffered allergy attacks in conjunction with pressure changes in the atmosphere. Their noses were better than any weather report, and always right on target. Usually, within twenty-four hours of an attack, it rained.

Glancing out the window above the bathtub, she looks at the sky. Though mostly bright blue, a few gray clouds are rolling in from the west. She guesses a storm will arrive by nightfall.

Running her fingers through her soft hair, she smiles while pulling it into a ponytail. "One step at a time, girl. One step at a time."

Grabbing her robe from the hook on the back of the door, she decides to beg Uncle Reed to make biscuits and his famous, mouth-watering gravy, for breakfast.

"Where in the hell is my cell?" She glances around the bedroom.

Setting the robe on the bed, she drops to her knees and checks under the bed, thinking the phone fell off the edge of the nightstand. She hears someone running down the hallway, followed by the front door slamming shut. She grins, glad she isn't the only one experiencing an irritating Saturday morning.

Seeing no sign of the phone, she rises and head to the living room. Uncle Reed is perched on the edge of the couch sipping coffee.

"Morning, Uncle Reed. Have you seen my phone?"

"Yes. It's right here. Come have a seat. Got some things I need to share with you."

"Oh, thanks! Mom would kill me if I lost another one." She reaches for the phone from its spot on the coffee table. "I swear I remember taking it to my room last night. Guess I inherited Mom's scatterbrain."

"Wait, Jesse. As I said, we need to talk."

Uncle Reed's hand clasps around her wrist, blocking her from the phone. The look on his face, and the gun on his hip, gives her pause. She senses something is wrong. "About what? Is Mom okay?"

"Yes." Reed softens the grip on her arm. "Your mom is fine. She's at the PD. Probably will be for a while."

"Well duh. Shifts are a full eight hours." She swallows the niggling feeling of worry and uses her mother's tactic of inappropriate humor in stressful situations.

"Sit. Now."

The tone in his voice makes the hairs stand erect on her neck and arms. She eases down next to him. "You must have started drinking decaf again, Uncle Reed. Lack of caffeine always makes you cranky."

"Funny girl, just like your mother." He forces a smile.

She takes a deep breath to control her nerves like she learned in rehab. "Don't take this the wrong way, but you look really worried. Why?"

Memories of when she was fifteen flashes by, recalling the morning she woke up and found her uncle sitting in almost the same spot, arms wrapped around her mom. The wounded, distant look on his face as her distraught mother broke the news her father had died in a car accident. The look on his face now is even worse. A lump of tears forms in her throat. "Wait…is this about Turner? Oh, my God! It is, isn't it? What happened to him? Did he get hurt while out hunting with his dad?"

"No, honey. This has nothing to do with him."

He pauses in mid-sentence as a weird rumbling noise from outside distracts his attention. In unison, they both turn and look out the window. Her mouth drops open upon seeing the line of camo-colored vehicles making their way down the street.

Before either of them has a chance to say a word, a loud voice announces, "Attention all residents of Hot Spring County. Per order of Governor Strickland, all citizens are to report to Malvern High School immediately. Those who refuse to comply will be forcibly removed from their homes. Repeating…all citizens are to report to Malvern High School. You have ten minutes. This is the only warning."

Shaking uncontrollably, Jesse pulls her gaze from the window.

Her uncle clears his throat. "As I said, what's going on has nothing to do with Turner. Your mother wanted me to keep you in the dark, but after that little spectacle, her request seems pointless."

"Keep me in the dark? About what? Why is our street full of troops, Uncle Reed? And why are we supposed to go to the high school?"

"I'm not quite sure just yet."

"Stop treating me like a fragile addict!" Her temper flares. "You and Mom have been tiptoeing around me for almost two years now and I'm sick of it. We were just ordered to leave, under the threat of basically being yanked from our homes if we don't comply, and I want—no, I deserve—to know why."

"You're right." He grabs the remote and turns on the television.

The annoying sound of the emergency broadcast warning blares through the speakers. The screen fills with the EBS emblem, noting it isn't a test. After the sounds of the warning end, the same instructions about heading to the nearest high school are given.

Throwing her hands in the air, she yanks the cell phone off the table and stands. "Well, that didn't answer my questions." With the click of a few buttons, she turns the phone on and soon, the sounds of multiple social media notifications fill the quiet living room.

Opening her favorite video sharing site, she clicks on the first one in her newsfeed. By the time she finishes watching it, her knees give out and she collapses onto the couch next to her uncle, stunned into silence.

Mouth dry and heart pounding, she watches one from Phoenix. Then another from Seattle. Mind already on overload, the one from her friend Megan's feed makes the room spin and her stomach quiver with disgust.

The video is from a rave in Memphis the night before. Megan's cousin had rented out an old warehouse downtown to throw a roll party to celebrate the holidays. Megan had stopped by two days prior and begged Jesse to go, asking her to be the designated driver to and from Memphis. Jesse resisted the temptation—even though it was extremely difficult—and told Megan she needed to find someone else.

She cannot get her mind to grasp she is looking at hundreds of dead bodies of former partygoers, some still clutching their glow sticks. The images are distorted because the person holding the cell phone runs through the crowd dodging bodies. The music is replaced by shrieks of terror. The multi-color strobe lights cast eerie shadows of the piles of the dead. Closing her eyes to the carnage, she prays Megan and her other friends made it out alive.

Tears stream down her face. She opens her eyes when Megan's voice shouts, "Dear God! They're eating people! Run!"

Blood and gore cover the still bodies and the ground. Several people crouch next to the dead. Her heart skips three beats while peering closer at the screen, praying that what she's seeing is a trick of the light, because it looks like something straight out of a horror movie.

"No...fucking...way...."

Ignoring her uncle, she drops the phone and runs to the bathroom, only making it to the door before throwing up.

Chapter 11 - This is Not a Drill

Saturday December 20th – 7:10 a.m.

DIRK KINCANON POWERS down the laptop and stares out the window. He needs a minute to pull himself together, so he watches the thick, gun-metal gray clouds swirl around in the sky. The ache in his bones warns a wicked storm is approaching.

Leaning back in the chair while rubbing his stiff shoulder, he takes a few deep breaths. Though still in great shape, he isn't the buff, twenty-something who'd enlisted in the Army almost thirty years prior. His body bears the scars from countless Special Forces missions as a former member of the 1st Battalion of the 20th SF Group headquartered in Birmingham, Alabama. His career in the military had taken him all over the world on covert operations. The horrors he'd witnessed dimmed in comparison to what was coming, and the thought made his stomach rumble.

Turning his attention to the eight-by-ten photo on the desk, he's hit with a pang of melancholy. Just as the photograph had been a source of inspiration for its previous owner, the happy family serves the same purpose for him now. The smiling faces of Jason and his wife and children stare back in silence. He'd retrieved the picture, along with everything he could stuff into his backpack, after scouring the lab for survivors.

That part of the mission had been pointless since all of them died.

He recalls the day he stormed into the facility almost one year prior. The bloody remains of his friend and others still haunts his dreams. He can never forgive himself for allowing Dr. Thomas to go to the lab alone. He shouldn't have ignored his gut instincts about Daryl Riverside, either. He tried to warn the good doc about the geeky bastard, and though Dr. Thomas listened to his concerns, he had nothing to offer as solid proof of his distrust of the scientist, so Dr. Thomas brought the boy into the fold.

Had he insisted on accompanying Jason to the lab, things would have turned out differently. Jason and Roberts would still be alive, and Dr. Berning wouldn't have turned into a complete and total shell of his former self.

Staring at the picture, his thoughts wander over to how he'd meet the only person he'd ever been close to other than his deceased twin brother. He'd been by Dr. Thomas' side ever since rescuing him from the jungles of El Salvador. Though he had been part of many ops to extract hapless civilians and dignitaries from around the world who'd found themselves trapped in hostile territory, the mission to retrieve Dr. Thomas changed the course of his life.

The shift in trajectory was partially from the loss of his entire unit nor from the tension-filled hours as he guided the nearly catatonic doctor through a haze of gunfire and explosions through the dense terrain. The other, bigger portion happened after rescuing Dr. Jason Thomas and the eight days they spent together surviving in the jungle. Something about the man's demeanor struck a nerve deep down in his darkened soul. Jason had endured being kidnapped by drug kingpin Mario Alvarado, along with his family, forced to attempt to keep the dying Mrs. Alvarado alive after complications during childbirth. The good doctor's mission of mercy as a member of Doctors Without Borders ended after being captured and skirted away at gunpoint by Alavardo's goons.

What really got under his hardened skin was Jason's sheer determination, which surprisingly, wasn't his will live or seeking revenge on the man who sliced his family up in front of his eyes. Jason was driven by an obsessive desire to make sure the world culled what he considered the source of all its problems—drugs and those who dealt them.

Huddled up together in the dark, loud jungle, Jason laid out his plans. Drug dealers ruled the world, paying off and even running some governments. The court systems around the world were helpless to stop or even attempt to contain the constant influx of cases stemming from drug charges. Prisons were overcrowded, and many jurisdictions bowed to social pressure to release offenders back into society.

Counseling didn't work. Rehabilitation centers had a combined success rate of non-relapse less than ten percent. Law enforcement agencies were outnumbered by the multitudes of dealers and struggled to keep up with the new, innovative ways drugs were smuggled into countries. The only solution, according to Jason, was to find a real, permanent cure to quell the cravings of addicts. His rationale was simple yet brilliant: If no one had a habit to feed any longer, drugs abuse would end, and dealers would disappear.

Dirk didn't pay much attention at first, assuming the ramblings were brought on by shock, exhaustion, and fear. Yet the more he listened to the intricate plan, the more he realized the scrawny man next to him wasn't crazy. Full of lofty, pie-in-the-sky goals maybe, but certainly sane.

After making it out of the jungle and to safety, the bond between the two was set in stone. At Jason's request, Dirk retired from the military and became the good doctor's full-time bodyguard. Once all the particulars were hammered out, he sought out and found the perfect location to set up shop in the Ozark Mountains. The cave was enormous and could easily house two hundred people with room to spare. Money was never an issue since Jason had married into money. His wife's vast wealth transferred over to her grieving spouse, and the man poured the funds into the project. The choice was the doctor's way of making sure the death of his family wasn't in vain.

They agreed to make the entire operation resemble a government installation. The idea was to make the scientists who joined believe their every movement was monitored, thus ensuring their full cooperation. In truth, they were monitored, just not by any government entity.

Dirk had been responsible for everything, including security and background checks, and on that end, he obviously failed.

Rising to his feet, he shakes off the continuous shame and humiliation that has been his constant companion for a year. There will be time to lament his mistakes later. Now, ensuring the safety of Dr. Berning and the rest of the small staff is the top priority.

From what he's witnessed on various news sites, including a live video feed from the Columbian Consulate in New York, things are deteriorating around the world at a phenomenal pace.

Dirk Kincanon has seen some fucked-up shit in his fifty-one years on the planet, but none of it compares to seeing the resurrection of the dead in front of his eyes, or the fact they seem to be hungry for human flesh.

Pushing all the mental crap aside, he lets his training take over. In less than three minutes, he is packed and ready. He leaves the bedroom and heads downstairs. In the hallway, he runs into Kevin Warton, a former Special Forces brother about sixteen years his junior. The look of concern on Kevin's face is proof enough he is aware of the situation.

"The lower quarters are secure, sir. I assume we're heading to the lab since it looks like a bio attack has happened?"

Taking the stairs two at a time, Dirk nods. "Yes. Have everyone ready to deploy in fifteen. We'll meet up in the garage. I'll drive Dr. Berning, and the rest of you each take a vehicle. Make sure to pack plenty of supplies. Enough for at least a year. If this is biological even that might not be enough."

"Already have three vehicles packed and ready, sir."

"Good job, Kevin. Always knew I could count on you." He pauses at the base of the stairs. "How are the others taking the news?"

"Best as can be expected. This crisis is the first time we've all been thankful to be loners. The only family we have left to protect is you and Dr. Berning."

"I know exactly what you mean. I'll round up Dr. Berning and secure his room. You take care of the others."

Kevin nods before veering left toward the main living area. Dirk walks down the long hallway toward Dr. Berning's quarters.

Rather than waste time knocking, he opens the door. "Dr. Berning, we need to…oh, looks like you already know."

Eyes full of worry and fear, Dr. Berning stands in the middle of his immaculate room, two suitcases by his side, dressed in an old pair of Kevin's Army fatigues, tufts of wispy gray hair poking out from the oversized cover on his head.

The elderly scientist looks like he's aged twenty years since Dirk saw him at dinner the night before. The once steady hands tremble, and his face is devoid of any discernable color.

"I'm afraid I do. I was watching the news until EBS cut in. After the first reports from New York and Memphis, I started packing, assuming you'd be down soon enough to retrieve me. Figured we wouldn't be making a trip to the local high school."

Stepping inside the room, he picks up the suitcases. "You are correct. Since we really don't know what type of contagion we're dealing with, it's best to get underground. The lab is full of all necessary equipment to keep us safe from any contamination."

"Agreed. Looks like whatever it is spreads fast. Plus, it seems a storm is brewing. I'd much rather hike to the lab while the ground isn't a slippery mess. Old legs, you know."

Dirk glances over the doctor's shoulder and sees light rain pelting the windows. "I believe, Dr. Berning, the storm already arrived."

Everett Berning nods in agreement before following Dirk out of the room, and he knows the old man understands the comment had nothing to do with the weather outside.

Chapter 12 - Attempted Containment

Saturday December 20th – 7:20 a.m.

REGINA'S TRAINING and instincts take over as fear pulses inside as fuel to her muscles. Turning on the lights and siren on the cruiser, she barrels out of the parking lot, damn near side-swiping a Humvee in a long line of others. Glancing in the rearview mirror to see if any of the vehicles changed direction and followed, she let out a sigh of relief as they ignored her and continued their trek to the high school.

Since the request for backup from Roger, the radio has been silent, which is even more unnerving than his terrified plea for help. An eerie sense of foreboding settles over her mind.

Lines of vehicles leading into downtown Malvern clog the southbound lane of Highway 270. The entire county is home to less than thirty-four thousand people, yet judging by the heavy congestion, it appears half of them are on the road. Some of the motorists she recognizes as residents of Rockport.

In less than two minutes, she crosses the bridge over I-30 and glances to the left. The accident shut down both lanes of the freeway; flashing blue strobes of numerous units dot the area, interspersed with red lights from a fire truck and ambulance. She looks right and notices a county unit blocks the interstate about one hundred yards away, holding back a throng of vehicles stretching for miles toward Benton.

Reaching the entrance ramp, she turns onto the freeway and pulls up behind a state trooper's unit. While scanning the area, a cold shiver races up her spine.

A jackknifed big rig is about one-hundred yards ahead, the contents of the trailer strewn across both the east and westbound lanes. A crumpled SUV nearly split in two is less than ten feet from the rig. Deflated airbags coated in red hang limply on the driver and passenger sides. What had once been a sedan of some sort is on its side in the median about twenty feet away. Glass, metal, and liquid cover the ground near the site of impact.

Up ahead about fifty yards sit Roger's and Clint's units, each empty.

"Where the hell is everyone?"

Leaving the car running, she steps out into the cold morning air, shotgun in hand. Pausing to listen, she hears nothing except the rumble of car engines in the distance. The eerie silence is unsettling. Accident scenes, especially ones involving numerous vehicles, are always a flurry of noise and activity.

Gas, burnt rubber, and the unmistakable odor of eviscerated bowels mix with the coppery scent of blood, making her nose twitch. She is used to the stench from working hundreds of accidents over the course of her career, yet each time she comes into contact with the foulness, her stomach twists into knots.

She considers trying to reach Roger or Clint on the radio, yet some primal instinct in the back of her mind urges her to remain quiet.

Raising the shotgun, she walks over to the unit in front of her, aiming steady and sure. The white Charger with blue stripes is about ten feet away, the driver's door wide open. No one is inside, so she continues toward the ambulance about fifteen yards ahead.

After passing the front of the cruiser, she stops after hearing a strange noise. Over the pounding of blood in her ears, the rumble of engines in the distance, and the mumbled voice of someone yelling through what she surmises is a bullhorn, it takes several seconds to recognize the sound.

Shifting her approach so she remains hidden by the open doors, she holds her breath, edging closer to the back of the ambulance, making sure to keep her steps quiet while sidestepping debris littered across the pavement.

The gurgling, crunching noises grow louder. Her stomach revolts, threatening to release its contents all over the freeway.

The world around her stops when she peeks around the open door into the interior of the ambulance.

Two mangled bodies, presumably victims from the wreck, are on gurneys in the back. The one on the left looks like a young female, maybe twenty. The right side of her head is crushed; glass and debris are deeply embedded in her neck. Mounds of blood has matted a once beautiful headful of dark hair. No more blood oozes from the injuries, indicating her heart no longer beats.

The other one is male. Both are strapped in, ready for transport to the hospital, IVs already in place. The man's face is a mutilated mess. His lower abdomen sports a gaping wound, and she can see part of his internal organs are exposed.

A large chunk of flesh is missing from his left forearm. She flashes back to the video of the accident on I-10 in Phoenix.

It looks like a bite.

Bile burns her throat upon realizing the man's jaw continues to open and close as he bites the air, his shattered teeth clicking together.

On the floor between them is an EMT, or what once had been one. The body cavity is ripped open, and a middle-aged woman dressed in jeans and a Texas Longhorn t-shirt, hovers over the corpse. She blinks twice in shock while watching the thing tear out a handful of intestines and shove them into her mouth.

Stunned, body and mind frozen in horror, the axis of her world shifts.

A human being is eating another human. A dead human being is trying to bite the air. Don't say it. Don't even fucking think it! No wonder the military is taking over and insisted everyone be tested. This...can't...be...happening. I've got to be at home, dreaming. God, please let me be experiencing a nightmare to end all nightmares.

In those few seconds while staring at things that simply cannot be, she's consumed with fear for Jesse and Reed. The two most important people in her life are in danger, along with, it seems, everyone else in the world. Her survival instincts take over, shoving all the disturbing sights and sounds aside to be dealt with later.

If this is a dream, it's time for me to kick some fucking ass.

"Hey, gut muncher? Want some fresher meat?"

The bloody monstrosity that used to be a living, breathing female jerks its head at the sound.

Regina notices the eyes are solid black and her skin a strange, mottled gray color. There is no humanity left in its expression; the dead eyes are primal. Crimson-covered lips ooze blood from its meal and curl back into a snarl. The thing hisses and lunges.

"Eat this!"

The recoil from the shotgun makes her entire body shake and ears ring from the blast. The body flies backward, smashing into the gurneys, and then crumples into a pile on the floor of the ambulance. The spray pattern from the shotgun at such close range removed ninety percent of her head, leaving only a few strips of flesh sticking up around the neck bone. Pausing only long enough to ensure the destroyed mass of flesh is dead—again—Regina pumps another round into the chamber and heads toward her men's vehicles.

"Always knew you was a smart gal, Chief. Take off the monster's head. It's the only way, just like in comics and movies. Who knew?"

Regina spins around at the sound of a familiar voice. "Jesus H. Christ, I damn near blew your head off, Clint!"

Officer Clint Chesterson stumbles forward before collapsing onto the cold pavement. Regina is by his side in seconds. The back of his dark blue jacket is shredded apart. Sections of his exposed skin are full of deep, ugly claw marks. Large chunks of flesh are missing where his kidneys are located. Blood soaks his shirt and pants.

Too much blood.

Bending down next to him, she looks at a pool of red mixed with saliva forming by his mouth. It spreads out across the ground, already the size of an orange. She scans the area for any more undead visitors and sees none, so she leans the shotgun against the ambulance and hoists Clint off the ground.

"Just hang on, son. I'll get you to the hospital as soon as I find Roger."

Clint spits out a mouthful of blood at the same time he tries to say something.

She doesn't ask him to repeat the words. "I'm gonna put you in the back seat for a minute until I secure the area. Any idea where he—and the others—might be?"

"Last time I saw him he was trying to help Hightower and Reynolds. They were on the backside of the semi. The driver was trapped inside, and they all were working to get him out. I was helping the EMTs load up the gurneys when I heard Roger yell for help. Took off running in their direction, but by the time I made it, well, shit went down fast."

Her mouth is cotton dry. She forces her lips to move. "Then what?"

"It was a waste of time. The guys were surrounded."

"Surrounded—by those things? How many? Are you saying you think Roger's dead?"

Clint groans as she leans him against the hood of her unit. Pausing long enough to grab the mic on her shoulder, she radios for backup.

No response other than the continual static. She tries again, requesting an ambulance.

Nothing.

Where the hell is Geenie?

After unlocking the back door, she eases Clint into the seat.

"Yeah, I think so." Clint groans. "There were four of those things surrounding them all. They all attacked at the same time. They were so fast...I took aim but didn't fire...afraid I'd shoot Roger. Right when one knocked him to the ground, I heard something behind me but turned around too late. It jumped me from behind."

"Oh, God. Did you kill it?"

He leans his head against the seat and winces. "Yeah, but not before he—it—whatever the hell you call it, tore me up. Unloaded my Glock until it quit tearing me apart. Found out taking its head off was the trick. Ha, just like on TV. Who knew those crazy people in Hollywood were right on the money?"

She watches as tears race down the boy's face. Clint's skin is pale and clammy. A fleeting memory of the day she interviewed him flashes by. He'd been just a few months' shy of turning twenty-two, all muscle and attitude, ready to get on the streets and make a difference in the community he'd grown up in. A former football star at Malvern High School, Clint Chesterson had been a textbook jock who skated through his classes while his teachers looked the other way when he turned in homework, obviously not a product of his own. Clint's sole focus was getting a football scholarship to Fayetteville to play for the Razorbacks.

The lifelong dream of the only son of Harold and Jeanie Chesterson ended the final game of his senior year after Clint suffered a torn ACL and broken left foot.

The image of him sitting across from her while he practically begged for a chance to have a real career makes her heart pound with grief. She had wanted to say no, tell him he wasn't ready, yet in the end, she caved. Something behind his big, brown eyes struck a sensitive spot inside her heart. Against her better judgment, she decided to give the kid a chance.

Now, as she stares at his life-ending injuries, she regrets the decision.

A gash about six inches starts at his temple and ends under his chin. The milky white sections of his skull and cheekbone are visible, and a steady stream of red leaks from it, dripping onto the collar of his jacket. She takes off her own and presses it against the wound before guiding his hands to take over. His breathing is short and hollow as his lungs fill with fluid.

After clearing his throat, he reaches out a bloodied hand and grabs her. She winces at how cold it feels against her warm skin. "From the sounds I heard from the others, they didn't make it either. Listen, I've got maybe half-hour, tops. Don't worry about me none. I've already made peace with my maker. After what I saw earlier, I ain't sure I want to stick around for what's coming next. Go, see if you can help others. Taking me to the hospital would be a wasted trip because I'm a goner. Just be careful, Chief. Those things are fast. And hungry."

"Don't talk like that, son. I'll get you to the hospital."

"No, you won't." Clint's grip intensified. "Promise me you'll get my parents outta here. Find Walter and Martha Addison. They'll know what to do. They've been waiting for this day to arrive for years. Please, Chief, don't let one of those monsters get to my mom and dad. Promise?"

She doesn't have time to answer Clint's request as movement to her right catches her attention. Shutting the door, she spins around and pulls her Glock, hands shaking while planting her feet and taking aim at the grotesque monster that once had been Officer Roger Singleton.

Son of a bitch. This ain't happening!

Tears run down her cheeks as she pulls the trigger, wondering how she'll tell Mary Louise Singleton she had to shoot her already-dead grandson in the head.

Before Roger's corpse hits the ground, the tornado siren breaks the silence. Stunned, she looks up into the cloudless sky, wondering if she's lost her mind, before returning her gaze back to her friend on the ground, choking back sobs as Roger bleeds out on the road. She forces herself not to succumb to the urge to collapse into a ball and cry.

Rather than running a full cycle, the wail cuts short, replaced by a robotic voice. "All residents of Hot Spring County are to report to Malvern High School. You have ten minutes to comply before house-to-house searches begin."

The message ends and the siren trills again, sending its loud sound waves across the expanse of Hot Spring County. She refuses to look at Roger's corpse and steps away from her car toward the fire truck up ahead. She can never forgive herself if she doesn't check on the others before leaving.

Her altruistic intentions vanish at the sight of several people—no, things—crossing the interstate, all heading toward the source of the noise blaring above them.

Regina's heart skips several beats.

Geenie.

The closest siren is less than one-hundred feet from the station.

She tries the radio on her shoulder.

The results are the same.

Nothing.

Regina focuses her gaze on the bloodied, strange moving bodies. The sun glints off the badges of two of them, and that is confirmation enough.

Spinning around, she jumps into the car. "Hang on, Clint. I'll get you to the hospital in a flash. Just hang on."

She glances in the rearview mirror; Clint's eyes are closed, hands still holding her jacket against his head. Clint responds with a slight nod. Jerking the wheel hard left, she makes a half turn and crosses the grass-covered median. Once on the other side and on the exit ramp, she floors it.

Back on 270, she slows down while navigating the throng of stalled vehicles. Some people stand outside or lean against their hoods, talking nervously to their fellow neighbors. Her stomach drops—they are in immense danger, and they don't have a clue.

Worried they might not be interested in additional instructions from the government, she opts for a different tactic. Turning on the outside speakers, she barks into the microphone, "This is Chief Parker of Rockport PD. Get back in your vehicles, roll up the windows and lock your doors. Right now! Danger coming from I-30 East. If you are armed, shoot the head. Repeat—shoot the head."

The reaction is immediate. Residents jump back into their vehicles, though a few hesitate while looking toward the freeway.

She makes it to the center lane and guns it. The hospital was less than three miles up ahead in the middle part of old downtown Malvern.

Unfortunately, the streets are barricaded and a large contingent of armed military personnel are in the way. They stand guard by the red light at the intersection of Cross and Highway 270, blocking the path to the hospital. Cars inch forward while IDs are checked before being allowed to proceed to the school.

"Shit." Regina whispers, immediately worrying Clint might have heard the fear in her voice. "Almost there, Clint."

The same sick, mewling grumble she heard on the freeway hits her ears. Before she has a chance to react, Clint's fingers poke through the partition, grabbing a handful of her hair. He pulls with such force her head smashes into the metal separating the front and back sections of the patrol car.

Slamming on the brakes, the change of momentum frees her from Clint's fingers after a large chunk of her hair rips out. In a state of panic, she slams the car into gear and jumps out.

She is greeted by a swarm of soldiers. One pulls her backward as another takes aim and fires. The glass shatters and Clint's head explodes all over the backseat and rear window. Screams of sheer terror erupt from the street as residents cringe in horror. Some flee on foot while others jump back into their vehicles and try leaving the gridlocked road.

Regina tries to intervene when the soldier who'd grabbed her raises his weapon, pointing it at an elderly woman ten feet away. The woman is dazed and confused, tears running down wrinkled cheeks as she stumbles toward the barricade, refusing to stop even when given the order to do so.

Without thinking about the consequences, Regina lunges forward and pushes the barrel of the gun toward the ground. Before she can say a word in protest, the soldier spins around and slams the butt of the gun directly to the side of her head.

The impact knocks her to the ground. Blackness with specks of white dots cloud her vision. She shakes her head, noticing blood spurts out onto the road, takes in a few gulps of cold air to regain her bearings, and ignores the throbbing pain.

Then, all hell breaks loose.

The soldiers turn on the crowd; guns pointing at their faces. Someone yells, "Oh, my God! Run! They're coming this way!"

Shots ring out in quick succession and the entire area descends into madness.

Regina stands and her knees get weak as a throng of the dead too large to count come over the rise from the freeway. The teeming mass isn't running but still moves fast. The soldiers forget all about the fleeing live bodies and concentrate on taking out the dead.

Lord, please take care of my family.

Regina pulls out her gun and runs to join the line of defense to protect her hometown.

Chapter 13 - Testing Commences

Saturday December 20th – 7:25 a.m.

REED STANDS IN THE middle of the small living room and stares at Jesse and Turner sitting on the couch, huddled together like one unit rather than two separate individuals. When the kid appeared at the door earlier, he looked terrified, but once inside and with Jesse damn near on his lap, the boy calmed down. For the last few minutes, Turner rambled nonstop, pausing only once when the tornado sirens blared, followed by instructions to leave.

Reed listened to Turner explain what his parents had planned, and how he wanted Jesse, and her family, to come with them. Reed is still chewing over all the information.

"Mr. Newberry?"

"Yes?"

"Are we going or staying?" Turner fidgets after trying to inject an authoritative air into his words.

"I'm not going anywhere or doing anything until Mom's here. Period. Uncle Reed, would you try calling her again please? My phone's dead."

Reed runs fingers through his hair as though the movement will somehow magically release an answer inside his head. "Jesse, the lines are jammed. Or down. Won't do any good to try again. Besides, she's probably swamped."

"Bullshit!" Jesse screams. "I'm not leaving without her. Let's just go to the station and ask her what she thinks, right now."

"Honey, we don't need to be on the streets. It's too dangerous."

Jesse shakes off Turner's arm, stands, and paces the floor like a caged lioness. Reed can tell she's close to a full meltdown.

"Don't, Turner...just...don't! God, this isn't real. It's an awful nightmare."

Reed swallows his own sense of dread. "Jesse, I know you're upset. We all are. We're in the middle of a situation none of us are ready to deal with."

"My family is, sir, if you don't mind me saying. We have a safe place to go, like I mentioned earlier."

He holds up his hand, silencing the kid. "We don't really know what all is happening, except for viewing some disturbing videos online and what we saw on the news."

"You forget the fact the freaking military just drove through town, and they instructed us to go to the school. They said we had to or else!" Jesse's voice cracks under the stress.

"Jesse—breathe. Your mom is doing her job, which is to protect the people of Rockport. My job is to protect you. So, I think since this..." Reed struggles to find the right words, "current situation is still in its infancy we should go to the school. If some disease is floating around in the air, we need to know, and take necessary precautions to keep from getting sick."

Turner's mouth drops open while staring at Reed as though he's crazy. "Are you serious? You're willing to put your lives in the hands of the government? When has that ever been a good idea?"

Shocked by the kid's sudden outburst, Reed's anger boils. Stepping forward, he angles himself in between Jesse and her boyfriend. "Look, I know you seem to think you know more than I do, but don't you dare take that tone with me. Ever. Do I make myself clear?"

His outburst is cut off when the front door bursts open and four men in full combat gear, including masks and loaded automatic rifles, storm into the house. Jesse screams and Turner jumps up from the couch, presumably, to put himself between her and the soldiers. The one closest to Turner barks, "Don't move or I will shoot."

"No need for all this." Reed keeps his tone casual, calm. "We were about to head to the school. Just discussing family business, that's all."

The one closest to him scowls. "Well, isn't that nice? We were just about to provide an armed escort. Remove your weapon slowly and set it on the table. Don't try anything or you will regret it."

Reed stiffens at the ominous tone, shocked he is being ordered by a fellow American—at gunpoint—to give up his weapon. "It's okay, sir. I'm U.S. Border Patrol, retired. Just trying to keep my family safe."

"I don't give a rat's ass if you're the Pope's brother. Remove the weapon. Now."

The thought of disarming himself makes his stomach quiver. For a brief second, he considers disobeying, but nixes the idea, afraid the wrong decision will put Jesse and Turner in jeopardy. With slow, calculated movements, he removes the gun and sets in on the coffee table.

"Smart choice. Any other firearms to declare before we pat you all down?"

Reed shakes his head. "Not on me, no."

"All of you raise your arms and lock your fingers together over your head."

The three comply and are patted down briskly by the soldier closest to them. Out of the corner of his eye, Reed notices Jesse's face is snow white. He fears she may suffer a panic attack any second.

Satisfied, the soldier who'd frisked them steps back to his original position by the window. The one in charge motions toward the door. "Move."

Jesse's crying from behind him. Turner looks terrified and furious at the same time, his light brown eyes shifting between Jesse and the soldier holding the rifle inches from his face. The boy's features harden as he clenches his jaw. The kid is about to make a stupid, stupid mistake.

Glancing at the nametag sewn in the fabric, Reed intervenes. "One question, Sergeant Russell, before we leave?"

"What?"

"Our phones aren't working, and I need to call my sister. She's the Chief of Police here in our town, and I told her I'd let her know when we left for the school. May I try calling her again before we leave?"

Sgt. Russell's expression remains the same. "If she is, then you'll get your chance to meet up with her later, after you've all been tested. Each of you have your IDs?"

Reed senses Turner is about to protest so he puts a hand on the kid's shoulder and squeezes. Their gazes meet, and Reed nonverbally conveys the message to be quiet and then answers, "We do, but my niece's is in her purse on the couch."

The sergeant motions toward one of his men closest to the couch, who picks up Jesse's purse and tosses it to Reed, who hands it to Jesse.

Grabbing her hand, he leads the way out into the bright morning sun. The chill in the air feels good against his flushed face. The uneasy feelings from earlier turned into a hot ember inside his gut. Glancing around the street, he notices the same scene played out in the front yards of his neighbors. At least ten Humvees are parked along the curbs of the street.

Jared McKay from across the street is arguing with his armed escorts, refusing to get into the Humvee. The old man is a World War II vet, pushing hard on ninety's door. A widower for nearly ten years, his only companion and reason to get up in the morning is his black Labrador, Oscar. Jared pleads with the soldiers at his doorstep, refusing to leave his dog. One of the men steps forward and shoves the tip of the rifle directly underneath the old man's chin. Jesse whimpers behind him, so he knows she's witnessing the same sight.

"Is that necessary? He's an old man—a veteran for God's sake!" Turner's voice rises. "One of your own! Maybe if someone explains to him what is going on."

"That's none of your concern." Sgt. Russell interrupts the outburst. "Mind your own business."

Though Reed feels the exact same way, he senses the sergeant, and the others with him, are wound tight. Glancing over to Turner he shakes his head, hoping the boy will keep quiet, but Turner's gaze is defiant and full of anger. The boy's once pale cheeks are flushed red from anger, but finally, he takes a deep breath and lets it out slowly while returning the nod.

They reach the curb where the Humvee idles. A woman's shrill screams pierce the air, and they all freeze.

Reed's mouth drops in shock. Two houses down, Stephen Sikes stumbles on the walkway from the front door and falls onto the pavement. The boy has been blind since birth and relies on his mother to guide him ever since his guide dog, Rollo, died six months prior. Stephen's family couldn't afford to purchase another. A fundraiser to help with the costs is ongoing, but slow to reach the amount needed.

Stephen's dark sunglasses are gone, his useless eyes nearly solid white. His movements are jerky and odd while trying to stand. A soldier closest to him raises his weapon and fires. The bullet tears through the boy's head and his frail body flops backward, landing at an odd angle on the ground.

The air filles with screams of agony and fury from the lips of his mother.

"Oh, my God! Stephen! No!" Turner yells. "Why? Oh, Jesus, why did they shoot him? He's blind for God sakes!"

"They killed poor Stephen! What in the world?" Jesse shrieks as her sharp fingernails dug into Reed's arm while clutching him in fright.

"You sorry bastards! That ain't right! He's just a kid who can't see! He posed no harm to anyone." Turner adds.

Reed feels the tip of the rifle press against his back, urging him forward.

"If y'all don't want to suffer the same fate, get in. We won't ask again. As I said before—mind your own business."

Jesse is crying so hard Reed and Turner must help her inside the vehicle. The doors shut and they began their journey to the high school.

Reed wonders if that is truly where they are heading while watching the remaining neighbors scurry inside the other Humvees. They look just as frightened on the outside as he feels on the inside. In all the years he's worked for the government, he never, ever thought he'd see the day when they treated fellow Americans in such atrocious ways.

With his left arm around Jesse's trembling shoulders, keeping the men in the front seats in his peripheral vision, he watches the chaos unfold on the streets. One man yanks poor Mrs. Sikes away from her son's body and shoves her into another Humvee.

The realization things are much worse than he imagined, and that they all are in grave danger from more than whatever disease lurks about, is sobering. He inches his hand inside his pants pocket and pulls out his cell, flicks it over to mute and clicks on the most recent text he sent the night before to Regina, pushes the microphone button and starts recording.

"Sir, what exactly are we being tested for at the school? Any idea how long the process will take and when we can return home?"

"Not in my job title. I'm instructed to round up everyone. Plain and simple. I'm sure someone higher up the chain will be able to answer all your questions, if they feel like it."

Jesse stiffens next to him. He swallows hard. "Why did your men shoot and kill Stephen Sikes? He wasn't sick—he just couldn't see and needed his mother's help."

"If you want to remain conscious for the remainder of the trip, keep your fucking mouth shut. Got it?"

Reed fights back the urge to lunge forward and beat the cold-hearted bastard to death or say anything further. He needs to keep cool and calm to protect Jesse and Turner. There is no telling what awaits them at the school. Worry spread throughout his mind, wondering exactly what sort of testing needs to be done to determine if they've been contaminated with whatever disease turned the world upside down in less than twenty-four hours.

Grinding his jaw, he nods as the vehicle turns onto the main highway and drives on the opposite side of the road toward downtown. He is shocked by the number of cars and trucks lining the road. Panic welled up inside him when he saw a Rockport PD Charger with its lights on blow past them. Though it passed by quickly, Reed can tell it is Regina. He glances at Jesse and breathes a sigh of relief. She is looking out the back window toward the freeway and missed her mother race by.

With the attention of the men otherwise engaged, he clicks stop on the recording then hits the send button, saying a silent prayer the phone lines work long enough for the message to make it to Regina's cell.

Thoughts of whether the cell towers are working vanish when Jesse screams, "What the hell is that?"

Turner and Reed both turn and peer out the back window.

The rumble of the Humvee's engine, the sounds of the cars, trucks, and people outside, disappear. For a split second, Reed's head swims with terror as he watches, mind pulled into the vortex of horror. A million thoughts race through his brain, each jockeying for control.

This isn't real. There's simply no way!

The Humvee screeches to a stop at the same time the familiar pop-pop-pop of gunfire explodes all around them. The sergeant barks orders at his men, who seem just as freaked out as the rest of the vehicle's occupants. The other three soldiers freeze, gaze nothing more than blank stares of sheer unbelief.

"I said move out! Now! Take these dead bastards down!"

In a flash, Reed, Jesse, and Turner are alone inside the Humvee, watching as the men join a group of other soldiers about forty yards away. The sound of multiple people firing weapons is deafening.

Turning back around, Reed faces the front, scans the area, and sees Regina's car skid to a stop about two hundred yards ahead. Black smoke rolls from the tires as the car turns sideways. The second the unit comes to a full stop; Regina jumps out from the driver's side. Fury barrels through him when she is yanked away from the vehicle by a soldier as another sprays her car with bullets.

Turner and Jesse are motionless next to him, rendered mute with fear. Reed glances at the dashboard. The second his eyes register he is looking at keys dangling from the ignition, he jumps into action. "Hang on!"

Shutting the driver's door, he pushes the button and locked the doors, turns the key, and smiles when the engine rumbles to life.

"What the hell are you doing, Uncle Reed?" Jesse gasps.

"Taking care of my business, that's what."

"About fucking time," Turner adds.

Ignoring the upstart, Reed slams the vehicle into gear and guns the engine, dodging numerous people scrambling for cover. In seconds, he stops next to Regina's unit.

"Stay here. Keep the doors locked and don't move until I get your mother. I mean it." Reed snatches the biggest knife he's ever seen from its sheath next to the driver's seat, leans over, hugs

Jesse's neck, and swipes her forehead with a quick kiss. "I'll be right back, honey. I love you. Turner?"

"Yes?"

"If things go sour, you take my niece to safety. I mean it."

Turner nods. "Yes, sir."

"Stop talking and go get Mom." Jesse mutters, shooing him out the door. "I need you both."

Knife in hand, Reed exits the Humvee, stepping out into utter chaos.

Chapter 14 - Time to Leave

Saturday December 20th – 7:35 a.m.

WALT ADDISON CRUMPLES the note Turner left in the middle of his bed, forcing himself to stay calm, yet he really wants to punch his fist through the wall. Better yet—smack his impetuous son upside the head, knocking some sense into his young brain. Part of him felt a sense of pride at his son's insistence on taking care of someone he loves, but a smaller part is furious he left to save a former junkie.

Even before Jesse Parker got strung out on drugs he never liked her because she was too headstrong and mouthy—just like her mother. He hates Regina Parker. Their falling out went all the way back to when she was Regina Newberry in grade school. She'd humiliated him at recess one sunny afternoon by kicking him in the nuts after he tried to kiss her. Walt had doubled over and threw up and then pissed himself in front of the entire school. He carried the nickname "Wee-Wee-Walter" for years, until he beat the shit out of enough people no one dared say it to his face.

The biggest worry gnawing inside his gut is how Martha will take the news about her only child's departure. He doubts his wife will pack up and leave without Turner.

Exiting the room after ensuring the windows are secure, he shuts the door behind and takes a deep breath while making his way downstairs.

"What's keeping Turner? We need to go, and I mean like right now. Lamar radioed in that troops took over the jail and saw a few Humvees heading this direction."

Knowing they don't have time to tiptoe around the issue of their AWOL child, he sighs. "He's gone."

Martha lets out a deep sigh, shoulders sagging. "I assume to get to Jesse?"

"Yes." He moves past her and grabs the bags next to the stairs.

"Can't say I'm surprised. Turner loves her."

"We can't wait for him to return if that's his plan." He heads toward the kitchen, his wife only a few steps behind. "He's a grown man who's made his choice whether we agree with it or not. We must go."

"He knows the way, right? He can make it to the cave without your guidance?"

Pausing at the door leading to the garage, he sets the bags down and faces Martha. He cups his rough, calloused hands around her soft cheeks. "I've trained him to the best of my abilities, honey. We both have. If he wants to survive this mess going on, he better recall what we've taught him. We always knew the day would come when he would leave the nest and go off on his own, right? Honestly, it's about damned time he manned up. Just wish he'd done it before the world went to shit."

Tears glisten behind Martha's eyes and to his surprise, she doesn't say anything. She simply nods and reaches into the bag on her shoulder, extracts two masks and hands one to him. He notes the tremors of worry in her hands.

Before securing it around his neck, he leans in and hugs her tight, closes his eyes and drinks in every smell inside their warm, inviting home, including the faint scent of Martha's shampoo mixes with her cherry body lotion and subtle hints of musk. The familiar fragrances make a lump of sadness form in his throat. A twinge of grief made his heart pound, wondering if they would return to the home they built together.

And whether their son will make it out alive.

Pulling away, he secures the mask while Martha does the same. Without another word, they grab the bags and slip into the garage, stow their belongings in the backseat of the truck, climb inside, and lock the doors.

Years ago, Walt cut out another wall in the garage and installed a separate door. Instead of opening to the driveway out front, the new one faces the dense woods of their backyard. He and Turner had worked for two straight months cutting down trees to make a path large enough for the tricked-out Dodge Ram to move through.

Walt starts the truck and smiles as the engine roars to life. Pushing the button on the opener, the metal door rises, exposing the brush-covered trail leading deep into the woods. Gunning the engine, the Ram shoots out into the bright sun. In seconds, the beams of morning light disappear as he drives them deeper into the thick woods.

Martha reaches over and turns on the CB, fiddling with the button until landing on the police channel. The sound of static fills the truck's interior.

Martha frowns. "That's odd. With all this craziness, you'd think the radio would be full of chatter."

He notices from his periphery Martha twisting the knob, attempting to locate anything.

The static speaks volumes.

"Try channel CB 3AM. See if you can raise Curt or Lamar."

Martha cocks her head and smirks. "I know the protocol, Walter. If silent, I move to CB 37U. If neither channel is operable, I switch over to the ARES to channel 34.90 so we can listen to what the National Guard is up to. I had a thorough teacher, remember?"

Hearing the tension in his wife's voice, he decides not to add more so he returns his concentration back to the bumpy road.

They are about one mile away from Bailey Hill, which means they'll pop out from under the cover of the woods soon. The only part of the journey that worries him is the short jaunt over the interstate. They will be exposed until they cross over to the other side, and the thought makes his stomach drop.

"Why don't you go ahead and switch over to the ham?" He slows down as the truck approaches an old creek bed. "I'd like to know if the troops are still in transit or already set up in town. I'm hoping for the later because I ain't looking forward to trying to sneak past them. Ol' Bubba here is a beast on the backroads, but sorta easy to spot in the open."

"How far are…oh, less than a mile. There, got it." Martha grins.

The static clears. "Sector A from Moss through Stone cleared. One casualty to report."

A different male voice responds, "Was casualty clear or contaminated?"

"Unknown. Squadron C handled it. They're right behind us, though their radio is on the fritz. They'll give a full report upon arrival."

"ETA and number of passengers?"

"Ten, tops. We're bringing in three—one female, two males. Elder male may be a problem. Former Border Patrol and related to local law enforcement. He's asking a lot of questions, and I don't think he'll remain cooperative for too much longer."

"Roger that. We'll be ready to handle him."

Walt slams on the brakes and halts the truck in the middle of the creek bed, turns, and faces his wife. The look on her face tells him she is thinking the same thing he is.

"Moss Street. That's the one Jesse lives on." Martha's voice is barely above a dry whisper while staring out the window.

He can tell she is scanning the woods for any signs of movement.

"Yeah. Looks like Turner won't be heading to the cave after all."

"Like hell he won't." Her jaw clenches and body tenses as she reaches behind the seat and grabs an assault rifle. Hauling it over the seatback, she flicks off the safety.

Despite the fear thrumming inside his mind, he smiles. Hell, high water, an armed soldier, or the hand of God himself doesn't stand a chance at deterring his wife once her mind is made up.

Shifting the truck into reverse, he backs up and changes destinations, driving back through the deep, muddy tracks he made minutes before, wondering if the trip into downtown Malvern will be their last.

The truck lumbers through the brush for less than fifty yards when the radio crackles to life.

"Big Bear, you there? Come back."

Martha snatches the mic up. "Lamar? Is that you?"

"Use our codes, Martha!" Walt admonishes.

"Please. Like it matters at this point!" Martha snaps back.

"Yes ma'am. Y'all already left?" Lamar asks, out of breath.

Walt detects fear in his friend's voice. "No. We had...a slight detour to make. Why?"

"We're about to be overrun by these things. I just stopped to catch my breath after running up the hill. I ain't even kidding when I say enough of them monsters are coming to fill up the parking lot of two Walmarts! They're moving in from the freeway, headed straight into town."

Motioning for Martha to hand him the mic, Walt asks, "You coming up Bailey Hill?"

"Yeah. About a quarter mile from the top."

"Stay put." Walt stops, puts the truck in reverse, and hands the mic Martha. "I'm almost there."

"Big Bear, is that your truck I hear?" Lamar asks.

"Yep. Can you see me yet?"

"Praise God!"

Lamar bursts from a clump of pine trees as Walt stops and Martha opens her door and Lamar jumps in. Walt puts the truck in gear and heads back to town.

Lamar is clearly shaken by the disturbing events. "All those people stuck in the traffic...Jesus, they were trapped! Those things overran the emergency personnel, too. The whole lot of them! Ain't never seen such in all my days!"

Walt and Martha exchange glances. Though worried, there is a spark of adrenaline-fueled excitement thrumming inside his body, and from the gleam behind Martha's eyes, she is feeling the same. "What mile marker, Lamar?"

"Ninety-eight."

"How fast they moving?"

"For dead people—pretty damned quick."

"Dead people?" Martha gasps. "What are you saying, Lamar? I thought this was a bio attack or contagious type outbreak of some sorts?"

"Ms. Martha, I ain't no doctor or expert on diseases-n-such. I just know what I saw out there on I-30."

"Which was?" Martha urges, doubt creeping into her voice.

"People who were dead stalking the living then eating them when they caught 'em. That's what."

"How do you know for sure they were dead, Lamar?" Walt queries, concerned about his friend's mental state. "I mean, you were quite a distance away. Maybe they just were injured."

"I see just fine through these." Lamar holds up a pair of binoculars. "And I'm fucking sure when someone's neck is snapped and their guts are hanging outta their body, they're dead. Even if they are still technically alive, I doubt they would be interested in eating the flesh off another person, don't you?"

"Dear God in Heaven." Martha clutches her hands to her chest.

Walt makes it to the edge of his property line, slows, pulls the truck over, and shuts it down. Without having to give instructions, they all exit. Walt and Martha open the crew cab door on their respective sides and grab their weapons.

"Time to change our outfits." Walt unzips the large backpack on the floorboard. Inside are three Kevlar vests and military fatigues. Glancing over at Lamar, he sizes him up. "Turner's a bit thinner than you so the vest might be snug, but I don't think being uncomfortable really matters at this point, right?"

Lamar shakes his head. "Hell no."

They change quickly. Once all three are fully armed, wearing similar outfits to their enemy, and masks in place, Walt moves to the front of the truck, motioning for them to come closer while leaning over and hiding the key under the front tire.

"We'll leave the truck here. Martha and I are gonna let the military handle the situation from the freeway. We were just heading back to get Turner when you hit us up, so if you want to go fight with the military, go."

Fury and sadness flash across Lamar's face. "If we weren't in the middle of a shitstorm, I'd punch you for that comment. I've been prepping my entire adult life to fight against the government, so there ain't no way I'd get on their side now! It's bad enough that I'm wearing clothes making me look like I'm one of them. Hell, hope Curt ain't out there somewhere, hiding in the shadows just waiting to pick them off. With my luck, he'd shoot me! So, you say they got your boy? How do you know for sure?"

"We heard it on the ham." Martha answers. "They're taking Turner, Jesse Parker, and Reed Newberry to the high school for testing. I don't like the idea of my boy being a pin cushion for the U.S. Military."

Walt huffs and pats the AR-10 resting by his side. "Darling, we got this. Ain't nothing more that scares the government than armed rednecks. Let's go get our boy and the others."

Martha nods before chambering a round.

Lamar frowns. "That used to be true until the dead started eating the living."

The trio only make it to the side of Walt and Martha's house before gunfire from across town shatters the stillness of the morning.

Chapter 15 - Addressing the Nation

Saturday December 20th – 9:25 a.m. – Eastern Standard Time

PRESIDENT ARTHUR THOMPSON closes his eyes and takes a deep, cleansing breath. He is a jumbled mass of fear on the inside but cannot let the terror shine through on his countenance. After a thorough debriefing by all his upper-level staff members earlier, and the reports he'd reviewed about the worldwide catastrophe, remaining calm is difficult.

Press Secretary Ari Newburg stands next to him in the ready room—close enough he smells fear wafting from his most trusted advisor. Ari's normally arrogant attitude had disappeared, along with his impeccable attire. The rotund man's gray suit is disheveled and beads of sweat glisten on his bald head and brow.

After the last three hours of briefings from across the globe, and the horrifying reports flooding in, he worries Ari is close to suffering another heart attack.

"They are ready for you, sir. Here are your notes."

He adjusts his tie. The pooling sweat underneath his shirt makes the skin itch. Taking the sheets of paper, he nods and opens the door.

The White House Press Room erupts with noise as reporters shout questions from the galley.

Unaccustomed to such obnoxious behavior, he forces himself to remain stoic and not wince at the onslaught. A sea of familiar faces—and a few new ones—scream for his attention. The room is packed and everyone on their feet. Two men near the front are covered in sweat, their faces pale, as they struggle to hold off the others from taking over their positions.

Holding up his hands to silence the crowd, he walks to the podium, waiting several seconds for the shouting voices to quiet down.

Looking down at the prepared notes, he grimaces. Something inside his mind whispers now is not the time to be politically correct. People are dying in droves across the world, and survivors do not need to have the news sugar-coated. They need solid, real answers and leadership to guide them through the unexpected, global crisis, so, instead of reading the prepared speech, he flips the notes over.

"Ladies and gentlemen, fellow Americans, and citizens of our world. It is with immense sadness I come to you today as our great nation and the entire world mourns the loss of so many lives. The terrifying events happening across the globe during the last twenty-four hours have left us all shell-shocked and fearful. We have witnessed scenes we never thought possible, and the images have caused us all to be scared.

"I am here today to assure you that the United States government is working diligently with the governments of every country around the world affected by the outbreak. What you need to know is the pandemic is not terrorist related. Though scientists have yet to isolate the cause, we do know what we are facing was not released upon humanity by any particular group. Now is not the time to let old prejudices and fears pervade our thoughts and attitudes toward others. Now is the time to unite as one collective group of humanity.

"Precautions must be taken to stem the spread of the disease. The CDC confirmed the disease only spreads through contact with bodily fluids such as blood and saliva. This contagion is not airborne and can only be contracted through contact with an infected individual, which includes being bitten.

"To ensure the safety of all citizens of our country, all fifty states are now under martial law. International and national air travel has been suspended, as well as interstate travel from state to state through any other means. As you have been informed by the Emergency Broadcast System, every single person must report to their local county seat where testing facilities have been erected. If you are traveling and not in your home state, please proceed to the closest county seat and present your identification for testing. Once tested and cleared, you will be required to remain inside the boundaries of the county until everyone has been tested. Please know we are working on a cure..."

His words are drowned out by a barrage of questions. Some of the staff writers from various news agencies around the world try pushing their way toward the podium. He attempts to regain control of the room but fails.

The voices from the crowd grow loud, demanding answers. They are more than panicked—they are hysterical. Some try pushing their way past the Secret Service agents standing in front of the podium. The two men he noticed earlier in the front aren't moving. They stand motionless, eyes glazed over as they stare at the floor. When the other reporters behind them crush forward, one of the men falls to his knees.

He doesn't stay down for long.

When the man jumps back up, President Thompson gasps upon seeing his eyes. They are solid black, no white or color visible, and the skin transformed into a dull, gray color. The blue of his veins makes weird, zigzag patterns underneath the skin. Crouching, his lips curled into a snarl, the man lunges and throws himself into the crowd.

The questions cease as the room fills with screams and the thunder of feet as people try to escape. The other sick looking man joins in the melee, grabbing the female reporter next to him and burying his teeth into her shoulder. In mere seconds, the once beautiful room is transformed into a horror chamber coated in blood.

The four agents in front of the podium open directly at the two monsters tearing apart the hapless reporters. The things move with lightning speed and before he even has time to blink, they descend on the agents, biting, clawing, ripping, and shredding the well-trained men into nothing more than bloody masses of flesh and bone.

Stunned, mind unwilling to accept the images flooding in, President Thompson freezes. Seeing the same scenes on a monitor earlier was disturbing enough, but experiencing a person ripping apart another only a few feet away like a wild animal is quite another.

Someone behind him grabs his jacket, yanking him backward until he's staring into the dark brown eyes of Ari Newburg.

"We need to go. Now."

All the years he's been the leader of the free world, Arthur Thompson never witnessed such chaos.

Then again, the world had never been overrun with the dead.

Once out in the hallway, Ari shuts the door to the press room and locks it. The sound-proof walls block the loud noises from the other side, allowing Arthur's ears a respite. Chief of Staff Roger Buffett runs down the hallway toward them, and the look on his face sends his own nerves further into overdrive.

Sweat droplets cover Roger's wide forehead. Tremors of fear make his hands shake as they reach out toward him. "You need to come with me. Right now, sir. Need to get you to PEOC."

Arthur refuses to budge from his position. In nearly eight years, he's never had to go underground to the Emergency Operations Center in the East Wing.

The request makes his stomach lurch. "I'm not going anywhere without my daughter. Where is she?"

Ari scowls. "Sir, the perimeter has been breached and our sole focus is your protection. Melissa will be fine. Agent Roseburg will take care of her."

"No, she won't. They are both gone." Roger clears his throat. "President Thompson, I'm sorry but we must go. Right fucking now!"

"Oh, my God. You're sure?" Tears blur his vision. "What happened? How?"

"Please, sir. We need to get you underground. Now." Roger urges. "I'll explain everything once you are safe. Now is not the time for this discussion. The world needs its leader safe. And alive."

The hallway spins as he's overwhelmed by the events of the last two minutes, mind teetering dangerously close to shutting down. Blood thrums in his head, making the sounds around him disappear. His heart physically aches at the loss of his daughter, and what is happening to the country he loves. Closing his eyes, he prays Melissa died of natural causes and doesn't turn into one of the living dead.

His gridlocked brain snaps to attention when a large group of Secret Service agents burst out of the Cabinet Room, forming a circle around him, Ari, and Roger with guns drawn.

"PEOC. Now!" Roger screams.

"Oh, shit!"

The hallway explodes in a clatter of gunfire. Ducking down inside the circle, Arthur clasps his hands over his head and waits for the deafening noise to end.

He doesn't have long to wait.

The gunfire stops, replaced with the wails of grown men screaming all around him. The one closest to him screams, "White House down! Jesus, White House down!"

The last thing he hears is someone yelling, "Shit, we can't stop them!"

President Arthur Reginald Thompson—graduate of Harvard, Vietnam veteran, husband, father, and leader of the greatest nation on earth—never has a chance to see what the agent closest to him is yelling about, because a bloodied hand reaches through the throng of dying agents on top of him and rips his eyes out.

Chapter 16 - Escape
Saturday December 20th – 8:30 a.m.

WALT, MARTHA, AND LAMAR flatten themselves in a ditch by the back of the high school; an eight-foot chain-link fence looming above them. Rather than exposing themselves by climbing it, Walt pulls a pair of clippers from his pack and in seconds, creates a hole big enough for the three of them to scoot through.

The back of the school is filled with Humvees. Scanning the perimeter, he saw no one. In a low crouch, the trio dash across the dead grass until reaching the door leading to the gym, which also serves as the cafeteria. Since it is the biggest, open area inside the building, he's sure that's where everyone is being held, but just to be sure, he peeks in the window.

He's right; the entire gymnasium is full of men and women in combat fatigues, masks in place, gloves on, lunch tables full of computers, lab equipment, and needles. Citizens are lined up in three rows: men, women, and children. The metal doors open, and a fresh group is shoved inside. A young couple cling to each other, trying to shield their infant daughter from the soldier's hands. The woman sobs and collapses onto the floor when a female in fatigues yanks the child from her arms.

Motioning for Lamar to hand him the binoculars, he scours the room, looking for Turner or the others. He spots Regina Parker first—and she isn't moving.

Her body is stretched out on a cot at the far edge of the room. The right side of her face is swollen, and she has several stitches closing a wide gash. Her eyes are shut; wrists bound by a set of handcuffs. She is unarmed.

Any other time, he would have chuckled at her predicament, assuming her smart mouth got her ass kicked, but not today.

At the end of the cot sits her twin brother and Turner. Both are pale, gazes darting around the room while watching their friends and neighbors stand in line to be tested. Reed Newberry has a bandage over his nose, swollen lip, and blood stains the front of his shirt.

Thankfully, Turner has no visible injuries. His boy sits motionless next to Reed, a look of fury and sadness beaming from his face. Walt says a silent prayer of thanks, grateful Turner is okay.

"Do you see him?" Martha whispers.

Walt nods and lowers himself into a crouch. "They got Chief Parker and her brother, too. Both look like they let their mouths get them into trouble. Parker's unconscious, and she's in cuffs."

"Well, that ain't good!" Lamar frowns. "You think she might be infected or something?"

"No. Other than being banged up, she looks fine."

"What about Jesse?"

"I didn't see her, honey."

Lamar scoots closer; back pressing tightly against the bricks. "So, how are we doing this? Storming in with guns blazing, or silent?"

"Silent." Martha answers first. "We've got to get them out without anyone realizing they're missing. And I know my son—he won't go anywhere until we find Jesse. I say we locate her first."

"Do you think maybe she tested positive, and they took her away?" Lamar asks.

His question hangs in the air like a thick cloud. Walt knows it is a distinct possibility, and he could tell Martha does, too.

The back door bursts open and two soldiers in full bio suits exit. In between them wriggles a screaming, terrified Jesse.

"I told you I'm not sick! The blood test confirmed it, so why are you taking me away?"

Oblivious to the trio crouched to their right, the two soldiers continued forward toward the closest Humvee. "We aren't taking any chances. You exhibit all the signs."

"I already explained. I have allergies, and that's why I'm sneezing, and my eyes are red!"

"Maybe so, but to be safe, we're taking you to the jail to keep watch for the next twenty-four hours. If you haven't turned by then, you'll be free to go."

As the soldiers walked further away, Walt can no longer make out what they are saying. It doesn't matter—they have the answer about what direction to take. Glancing at the back door, which is still open, he raises his arm and points. The trio stand and slip inside the kitchen, undetected.

No one else is inside the room, so they ease forward until reaching the double doors leading to the cafeteria.

"Walk with a purpose yet try to avoid speaking to anyone. Follow my lead." Walt's voice is barely above a husky whisper. "We'll head straight over to get Turner, Reed, and Regina. That little spectacle with Jesse will help. We'll lead them out this way, and if anyone asks what's going on, I'll handle it. Got it?"

Martha and Lamar each nod in agreement before stepping through the doors.

The sound of terrified voices—some crying and others yelling—fills the gym. Walt's heart thunders in his chest. Their presence goes unnoticed as they make their way across the room over to Turner.

Walt is first to reach his son. Turner looks up, eyes full of rage until realizing he is staring at his father. Turner's gaze shifts between his mother and Lamar, and though he doesn't smile, his eyes reflect immense gratitude and relief.

Glancing around to make sure they are out of earshot of the others; Walt lowers his head. "We're getting y'all outta here. It ain't gonna be easy, so forgive me for what I'm about to say. Now, both of you get her up and take a side. Head toward the kitchen."

Reed nods and rises. Turner follows, and in seconds, they hoist Regina's limp body off the cot. She groans but doesn't wake up.

Walt steps aside and lets the men lug Regina past him. The trio fall into steps behind them. They are close to half-way when a voice behind them queries, "What the hell are you doing?"

Stopping, Walt turns around and faces a soldier no older than Turner. The kid's features, except his eyes, are hidden by a mask. The boy's dark brown eyes reflect his struggle to remain calm.

"Taking them to jail. A family member tested positive, so to be safe, we're going to quarantine the entire family. Can't afford any to slip through the cracks, right?"

The kid takes several steps backward. "Oh, okay. Good idea. Best to be cautious, that's for sure."

Walt gives the boy a nod and the group continues forward. When they reach the door to the kitchen, their sense of accomplishment is short lived.

"Oh, my God!" someone screams.

"Run!" another yells.

The cafeteria erupts into chaos. People scattered…and they are all heading toward the kitchen.

"What the hell?" Martha asks.

Her answer is a barrage of gunfire.

"Jesus, some made it in here!" Turner yells.

Wals shoves the door open. "Move! Now! Follow me!"

The group runs through the kitchen. Whether it is the noise or movement that does the trick, Regina wakes up. Without a sound, Reed and Turner let go, and they burst through the back door.

"This way, come on!" Walt instructs.

The six of them barely make it twenty yards before a stream of panicked people exit the doors. The back parking lot fills with hundreds of bodies—some living, some dead—in seconds. People shrieking from terror drown out the sounds of their feet on the blacktop.

"Through here!" Walt grabs the section of fence he'd cut through earlier and pulls back. "Hurry!"

Lamar is the last one to go through. His weapon catches in the links of metal. Pausing to free it, he isn't looking behind him, but Walt is, and what he sees makes his guts rumble and head spin with doubt and fright.

"Don't move!" Walt yells at the same time as he raises his weapon.

The crackle of bullets joins the screaming of others as he blows the head off what once had been human.

The thing collapsed inches from Lamar's leg. "Fuck this!" Lamar yanks one more time, freeing the AR-10, and then crawls to freedom on the other side of the fence.

The six of them run deep into the woods, each breathing hard. After about fifty yards, Walt changes course and heads east.

"Where're we going?" Martha asks.

Ignoring his wife, he continues running. They need to put a lot of distance between themselves and the school.

After another few minutes, Reed yells from behind him. "Wait! Stop! We're clear now."

Walt looks behind him and notices Reed is right. They are about one hundred yards deep into the forest, and no one or thing is behind them. The sound of the siege at the school has stopped.

"Where's Jesse?" Regina clutches her side. The stitches on her head ripped open and fresh blood drips down her face and neck.

"They took her to the jail." Martha sighs.

"What? Why? Is she…?"

"No, sis. Jesse's fine." Reed's voice is smooth and steady, which Walt finds odd during such chaos. "She had an allergy attack this morning, and they assumed she was infected."

"Thank God."

Walt doesn't even try hiding sarcasm from his tone. "What did you say to the grunts to make them knock you out? Question their authority or something?"

"That story is for another time, Walter." Regina retorts.

He caught a glimpse of anger behind her eyes, but it disappeared as quickly as it arrived. "What's really going on, Chief? Ebola? Smallpox? The Plague? Any idea how it's spreading?"

"I don't know. From what I've seen, it's a combination of anything and everything. The only thing I know for sure is if you get bitten, you—well, not sure how to describe it. Turn I guess is the best way to put it. Oh, and I got an email from the Governor earlier, warning all personnel to wear bio suits. Contaminated people are to be taken to the jail."

"I don't understand, Chief. Why not the hospital?" Martha interjects. "The jail doesn't have the resources necessary to help anyone."

"My guess is because there isn't a way to stop the progression once infected. They turn fast and don't stop unless you destroy the brain. They can keep them behind bars at the jail."

"For what purpose?" Turner asks.

"Not a clue." Regina turns her focus to Walt and Martha. "Okay, so I'm gonna say this once and fast. Walt, Martha, Lamar—thank you for saving us and telling me where to find my daughter. Walt, before I go get her, I need to ask you to do something for Clint Chesterson. I made a promise to him."

"Is he dead?"

"Yes. So is Roger. Clint wanted you to get his parents to safety. He said you and Martha were the best—and beyond prepared for whatever the hell is going on."

Walt nods toward Turner. "Come on, son. We need to get to Ol' Bubba and then head to the Chesterson's."

"No, Dad. I'm going with Chief Parker."

The boy from hours ago is gone, replaced by the hardness of a man. He'd seen it happen to young men during the war—dire situations with death the result burns away youth in a flash. The defiance in Turner's eyes speaks volumes.

"We all are going with the Chief." Martha's tone is stern and commanding. "This ain't the time to split up into splinter groups. Safety in numbers, remember? Then, once we gather up everyone, we're getting the hell out of this town."

Mouth agape, he stares at his wife, considers protesting, but knows she is right.

As always.

"Chief, let me get those cuffs off you and patch you up first." Martha scrounges inside her pack for medical supplies. "You got your key on you still?"

"Yes, right front pocket."

"Perfect. Let's do this. Can't have you bleeding all over. I imagine those things are attracted to the smell of blood."

Regina nods, glancing behind her toward the school. "Yeah, and noise. Time to end this conversation and approach the jail in silence."

Five heads bob in agreement.

With the precision of a nurse, Martha covers the wound to Regina's head in seconds. They all stare at each other knowing they are about to embark on a mission that may end with all of them dead, whether from the military or the diseased corpses.

Turner takes off first. The rest follow as they run toward the jail.

***

Benito's entire body aches. The pounding in his head makes his stomach queasy and vision blur. He tries sitting but his muscles refuse to cooperate. Blinking twice, he takes a deep breath and nearly cries out when burning pain tears through his chest from what he fears are broken ribs. Taking shorter, smaller breaths, he tries to keep from panicking.

The last thing he remembers was being in the air with Fernando as they approached the landing strip at the edge of the estate. Fernando started convulsing and the helicopter took a nosedive. While prying Fernando's fingers from the controls, Fernando tried to bite him.

Infuriated, terrified, and not thinking about the consequences of killing the pilot, Benito pulled his gun and shot Fernando between eyes. As the helicopter's warning system blared, he tried regaining control of the chopper but failed. The ground rushed up and then everything went dark.

The images and sounds from earlier while on top of the building in San Salvador slam into his mind and he shivers. He is an easy target if any of those things from the city made it this far, so he forces his body to obey his mind, stands, and winces in pain. His left arm hangs limply at his side. He's unsure if it is broken or dislocated, and really doesn't care. At least it is his arm and not a leg.

After taking a few tentative steps, something warm runs down his side so he stops, pulls up the tattered shirt, and curses under his breath upon seeing the long gash about the length of his hand above the right hipbone. It doesn't seem too deep yet it's bleeding profusely. He cannot move his other arm, so taking off his shirt to use as a tourniquet is impossible. He tries ripping a section off from the bottom but lacks the strength to tear the material.

With nothing left to use, he lets the shirt back down and clamps the good hand over the folds of torn skin, biting his bottom lip to keep from screaming while crushing the split edges together.

Looking around, he squints. The morning sun hurt his eyes. He glances to the left and sees the mangled remains of the chopper about twenty yards away. Pieces of what had once been Fernando are strewn across the tarmac.

Stumbling toward the main house, he is shocked he survived the crash. He tries recalling how he extracted himself from the chopper before impact but cannot remember. At this point, it doesn't really matter. What matters is getting inside the brick fortress and barricading himself inside.

Pace slow, it takes him nearly fifteen minutes to make it to the back gate. He curses while looking at the brick wall, which is over fifteen feet high. In his current condition, there is no way for him to scale it. Shuffling over to the wrought iron gate, he prays it is unlocked, though he knows it will be.

Sure enough, it doesn't budge when he attempts to open it.

He leans against the hot bricks of the wall as a wave of dizziness from extreme heat and intense pain forces him to pause and catch his breath. There is no other way inside except one: push the buzzer and have one of his men unlock the gate from the inside.

He will not risk his men seeing him vulnerable because that is just as much of a death sentence as remaining exposed outside the walls.

Mario's words from the night he killed him replay over in his mind.

"You may ascend to the top now, but one day, you'll be the old dog. The pack is full of scheming members just waiting for the time to strike. They may bow to your whims now, drooling over whatever reward you dangled in front of them to betray me. Yet one day—just as you've done—they'll turn and sink their teeth into you."

His anger flares. The ominous warning from Mario was right on target. Even though he's barely clinging to consciousness, he cannot risk entering the estate when so weak. There is only one other place he can think of—the stables.

Forcing himself to continue moving, he heads to the stables. There is medicine and bandages for the horses inside the office. He could patch himself up and rest long enough to regain much needed strength. Glancing over to the closed-circuit camera facing the gate, he smiles. It isn't on, which means the men inside have no idea he is outside.

Using the brick wall as a shield, he hugs it closely, making his way toward safety. Struggling to stay on his feet from the intense pain, he recalls the tricks he'd learned to block the physical and mental pain when Mario abused him. He forced his mind to believe he was climbing a mountain and at the top was an enormous treasure chest stuffed full of everything he'd ever wished for. Each painful second pushed him closer to the peak, and the rewards would outweigh the excruciating journey.

This time, instead of picturing a treasure chest on top of a mountain, he imagines himself back on the rooftop, watching from his perch as the streets of San Salvador fill with beautiful, naked women strolling down the cobblestone streets toward him, converge at the condo and dance their way up to the roof. One by one, each woman descends on him until the hundreds of naked torsos became one writhing pile of sensuality with him in the middle, body in a constant state of orgasmic bliss as the wenches' stroke, rub, caress, and suck him dry.

By the time he reaches the big door, he is exhausted from the mental jousting. It takes two tries to slide open the door and step inside but once he does, he's grateful the place shields him from the burning sun.

The barn houses six horses, all Maria's. Well, not anymore. Now the beautiful Arabians are his, though now, he doesn't care. They are leftovers from Mario—gifts to his headstrong daughter to help placate her constant state of boredom. He figures they are hungry and again, doesn't care. Taking care of the beasts had never been his responsibility, and it certainly wasn't on his agenda now. As he shuffles his way down the aisle, he considers letting them starve inside their stalls. Though tempting, he decides to let them live—at least long enough to retain some muscle. If things continue to go downhill in the world, horsemeat is quite tasty and a good source of protein.

Ignoring their collective whinnying at his appearance, he continues until reaching the office.

The door is locked, so he grabs a shovel leaning against one of the stalls to his right, groaning in pain with the movement. He smashes the glass covering the top half of the door, reaches in, and turns the deadbolt. Once inside, he removes the key to the medicine cabinet from the top desk drawer.

Grabbing everything he can use, he sets about cleaning and caring for the injuries. The first thing he does is chew up a handful of aspirin, hoping it will kick in soon and help ease the pain. The bitter pills make him gag yet he manages to keep them down.

He struggles with opening the lid on the hydrogen peroxide but is successful after several attempts. He rips open the plastic housing a fresh bandage and then pulls up the shirt. The wound seeps bright, red blood.

Fearful he may faint when dousing the wound with medicine, he concludes it will be best to lie down on the desk. It takes him a few seconds to clear the top and get himself situated. Once ready, hands shaking from the upcoming pain, he closes his eyes and takes his mind back to the rooftop of throbbing pussy, and then pours.

For the first few seconds after the cold liquid hits, he keeps his mouth closed while his body shakes as though being electrocuted. After holding out as long as possible, a feral scream erupts from his throat.

Unable to stand the pain, he throws the bottle across the room; chest heaving for air. Blackness fills his vision and threatens to swallow him in a dark vortex. It is in this precise moment something sparks to life inside his mind about the crash.

Fernando arrived a little before 1:30 a.m. He doesn't know what time it is now but guesses early morning, perhaps eight or nine. The mansion is less than half-an-hour's ride from San Salvador, which means the chopper crashed sometime between two and two-thirty a.m., which means he's been unconscious for hours less than half-a-mile from the estate's main gate4.

Why hasn't anyone come to help? Where are his men? The main house is big, but not soundproof. A chopper could be heard approaching, and even if the men were in a state of panic from watching the world fall apart on the news or web, they couldn't have missed the noise from a helicopter crashing.

While wrapping the bandage around the cleansed wound, he grapples with two possible scenarios inside his mind. Did his men flee like cowards at the first sign of trouble? That would explain why no one came to investigate the crash site. The other idea rumbling inside his head makes his stomach tremble. What if one of them decided to party and snorted some tainted coke? If even one of them turned…

Pushing the disturbing second scenario away, he focuses on the task of dressing the wound while silently cursing the whereabouts of his men. The horses grow louder and a few stomps and snorts in their stalls, making it difficult for him to concentrate.

"Necesito que te calles!"

Bandage secure and mind racing, he rises from the desk, fighting back a wave of dizziness.

He shouldn't have ignored the warnings of the horses.

His instincts sense a presence behind him before his mind has a chance to grasp, he is in danger. The hairs on his neck and arms stand erect in response. Weird, gurgling sounds come from multiple positions behind him. Swallowing hard, he grabs the scissors to his right and spins around—and discovers the answer to his men's whereabouts.

He raises the scissors about his head. "Me cago en la leche!"

Benito San Nicholas—possibly the only man left on the planet who know exactly how society fell and why, and the man responsible for ushering in the end of the world—never has a chance to inflict any damage or make another sound because his dead, hungry former foot soldiers never give him the chance.

Chapter 17 - Breaking Out

REGINA AND THE OTHERS crouch behind a Humvee and watch the jail. They had stopped once on their way and quickly changed clothes. She had removed her uniform shirt and Turner now wore it under his sweatshirt. Reed had taken off his undershirt and given it to her and then switched outfits with Walt.

The soldiers standing guard at the front entrance to the jail look edgy as they pace around, one huffing away on a cigarette, all their attention focused east. The gunfire from the highway and school had trickled down to short, random bursts instead of steady pops.

Either they were winning the battle, or…Regina pushes the thought aside. "Okay, we ready?"

Reed nods and pulls the mask over his face. "Yep."

"I can't believe I had to wait until the end of the world happened before I got a chance to see you go to jail." Walt snickers.

She turns and looks at him, wondering how much of his comment is a simple joke to ease the tension and how much is truth. She is aware Wee-Wee Walt Addison holds no warm, fuzzy feelings for her. "The apocalypse makes strange bedfellows, that's for sure."

"Stop wasting time! Let's get in there and get Jesse!" Turner's voice is low yet tinged with borderline hysteria.

Walt kisses his wife long and hard. "Be safe, lover."

"Always. Let's go."

Walt and Lamar remain in their spots while Regina, Reed, Turner, and Martha stand and walk across the blacktop toward the jail. Regina and Turner put their hands behind their backs as though handcuffed as Reed and Martha march behind them.

The sounds of their footsteps cause the four men guarding the entrance take note. Each raise their weapons and move in unison to the front of the glass doors leading inside. The man closest to them who'd been smoking only seconds before laughs.

The devilish sound sends a chill up Regina's spine because it isn't anything close to humorous.

"Two more? Jesus, they're coming outta the woodwork!"

"I don't know why we're wasting time and risking our lives for soon to be corpses."

"That ain't our call, boys. We're just following orders like everyone else." Reed keeps his expression unreadable. "There's more at the school we need to fetch, so the sooner we get these two secured, the faster we can help the others. We're spread thin after all the fighting."

"No doubt. The standoff in Rockport was scary. Knew if those things made it past the barricades, we'd all be in serious trouble."

Regina's heart thuds in double time. She hoped Reed would ask about the status of the attack near the interstate, and she wants to hug him.

Reed continues. "We were at the school and missed it. Were y'all there?"

"Yep. I tell you, when the police department was overrun, I thought we'd lost the battle. Then after we hit it with several grenades and the explosion happened and boom! Sent a whole mess of the dead back to hell where they belong. Gave us time to take out as many as we could see. Damn those things move fast."

Even though Regina's head is down, she keeps her face calm and expressionless. Inside her mind, she whispers a silent prayer for Geenie. *God love her.*

The four men seem to buy the charade and step away from the entrance, allowing enough room between them for the foursome to pass through. One even opens the door and then stands back, she assumes, because he doesn't want to get any closer for fear of contamination.

They make it inside the jail and the tightness in her jaw relaxes upon realizing the reception area is empty and the closed-circuit cameras lining the back of the desk are unmanned. She told Reed, Martha, and Turner prior to arrival to maintain the façade of guards and prisoners in case they were being monitored by the security cameras.

Hot Spring County jail is large considering the minimal population of the county, yet small in terms of actual size. It can house up to a maximum of fifty inmates, and since she knows the layout, she takes the lead.

Upon arriving at the first set of locked doors, her heart sinks.

Three armed guards and two Hot Spring County deputies block their way, sitting around the desk housing the controls to the bars on the other side. Regina keeps her head down and prays Deputies Jackson Allsop and Mike Bailey don't recognize her, thankful the side of her head is bandaged, and she isn't wearing her uniform.

The guard sitting closest to them groans. "We ain't got room for more."

"Not our problem. Sergeant Russell gave orders for us to bring them here." Reed's voice bellows across the expanse of the room.

Though doubtful anyone else heard the fear in her brother's voice, she did, and can tell he is thinking the same thing she is: if there isn't any more room, what are they doing with the sick?

"I don't care what the Sarge said, we're full up! Besides, we take our orders from Lt. Pack, and he said to take any new arrivals out back and terminate them."

"What?" Martha gasps. "We're just going to kill them in cold blood?"

"Better them than us, right? We're under Martial Law now. Y'all arrived just in time. We were just giving orders to take the ones already inside out back. We'll need the extra help getting them outside and burning the bodies."

Regina cannot take any more callous behavior. She looks up and straight into the faces of Allsop and Bailey. They appear terrified yet unwilling to attempt a coup on their own. Considering they are outnumbered; she cannot really blame them. She hopes that is really the case and that the men she'd known for years hadn't turned into cold-hearted monsters so quickly.

Seconds ago, she hoped they wouldn't recognize her, but that changed in a nanosecond.

Searching their faces for any signs of recognition, she is greeted by blank stares. Unwilling to let the others know she isn't really handcuffed; she remains still, speaking directly to Allsop and Bailey. "My daughter's in there, sick like me. Please, let us be together when you kill us. I don't want to turn into one of those things, and I know Jesse doesn't want that either. Just allow us to hold each other one last time?"

The silence inside the jail is eerie. Five sets of eyes stare at her, three full of hatred and anger, but the two deputies she hoped to reach fill with pity, sadness, and then recognition.

A spark of hope appears on Allsop's face. He gives a slight nod before reaching down and pushing the button, unlocking the bars.

"What are you doing you fool?"

On cue, Allsop, Bailey, Reed, and Martha turn their guns on the three soldiers. The men freeze, giving Regina time to burst through the open door and grab the automatic rifle of the one closest to her position, and the look on his face after she snatches it away would have been comical under different circumstances.

"Sorry, Chief. Didn't recognize you for a second." Deputy Allsop lets his breath. "You okay?"

"Don't worry, boys." She nods, a hint of a wicked smile touching the corners of her mouth. "I ain't sick. Neither is Jesse. We're here to get her out, that's all. What cell number is she in?"

"Seventeen, Block B." Deputy Bailey's gaze never leaves the three soldiers. "Don't worry, none, Chief. I've known your little girl since she was a baby. Could tell she was just having one of her allergy attacks. I made sure they put her in a cell by herself."

"Bailey, you're a gem. Now, let's get these boys here secured. Make sure to take their radios. Don't need anybody calling for backup while we break my kid out of jail."

"Gladly." Martha moves quickly and, in a flash, handcuffs all three soldiers.

Regina stifles a chuckle. Martha Addison seems to be enjoying her new role.

"You'll pay for this once Lt. Pack hears what you've done."

"That may be true later, but not right now." Regina stares into the eyes of the man who'd been talking to them earlier. "You mentioned we are under Martial Law, right?"

"Yep, so when I'm able, I'm gonna kick your ass!"

Regina smashes the butt of the rifle into the bastard's nose. The sound of cartilage and bone crunching fill the small area. Blood shoots from the soldier's nose as his body tumbles backward over a chair.

"Any of you other heartless fuckers have anything to say?" Regina addresses the other two men, who immediately shake their heads. "Good, because I'm done playing nice with the military."

Reed steps forward, motioning for the two men to get on the ground. "Sis, go get Jesse. Martha and I will make sure these boys stay right here."

Deputy Bailey pushes a button on the console and the metal door slide back. Allsop yanks a set of keys from the limp body of the soldier with the broken nose. "I'll be taking my keys back now. Bastard."

Regina leads the way, Turner, Allsop, and Bailey flanking her, and they step through the entryway and head into the center of the jail, only making it three steps when the sounds of mewing and groans from the cells up ahead hit them.

"What the hell is that noise? And that horrible stench?" Allsop crinkles his nose.

"That would be from those who've turned. You know, dead people who smell your blood or hear us. God, that doesn't sound right. The dead smelling and hearing." Regina holds rifle steady, gaze tracking for any movement. "Stay in the middle of the aisle, away from the bars. They are strong, hungry, and determined."

"Holy God, what a nightmare."

"I know, Bailey. Keep moving." Regina urgers. "We're almost to Block B."

Ignoring the rising noise from former residents of Hot Spring County as they grunt and clang on the bars of the cells, she stops, letting Allsop move ahead.

The second he inserts the key unlock the door; the sound of Jesse's screams send waves of terror inside Regina's heart. "Open that fucking door!"

Allsop swings the door open, and the group lets out a collective gasp when they come face to face with what used to be Sheriff Roger Calhoun.

***

Jesse rubs her shoulders while pacing inside the small cell to keep warm, wishing she had a jacket and boots, but there wasn't time to change when the soldiers forced them from the house. The thin pajamas and slippers were fine inside a warm house, but not inside a cell with concrete floor and no source of heat.

She hadn't been behind bars since Fayetteville. Being trapped in the confined space is a nightmare on its own, transporting her back to a time in her life she never wants to revisit. With the added stress of everything else going on, it is too much for her mind to grasp.

She's tried every trick she knows to keep from having a panic attack during the last two hours as terror and adrenaline took over her thoughts after watching Stephen Sikes gunned down like an animal. After seeing the amount of dead people converge onto the streets of Rockport, she'd gone numb while Uncle Reed drove the Humvee away before leaving to go find her mom. She'd clung to Turner for support, and thankfully, being near him helped keep her from flipping out.

But that didn't last for long because things went from bad to worse. People ran screaming from the onslaught of the dead and deafening gunfire. She tried to keep Uncle Reed in her sights but lost him in the crowd. She had started crying again, overcome with worry she wouldn't see her mom or uncle again.

Though time seemed to have stood still while watching things that simply could not be happening, she guessed about three minutes later when Uncle Reed burst through the crowd carrying her mother's limp body over his shoulder. Jesse had scrambled to unlock the back door to let him in, but the second Uncle Reed set her mother in the back seat, her face covered in blood, two soldiers rushed the Humvee. One of them grabbed Uncle Reed's collar, smashing his face into the doorframe, which knocked him unconscious. Before Jesse had time to grasp what was happening, the other soldier stuck his rifle in Turner's face, forcing him to move. In minutes, they were at the high school.

Uncle Reed and Turner carried her unconscious mother inside, and a female soldier dressed her wound, and being near her mother helped her calm down, but then she started sneezing again and two men grabbed her from behind. Turner tried to stop them but was forced to remain seated by two armed guards.

The soldiers took Jesse to the end of a long line of lunch tables. A female soldier drew her blood and deposited a few droplets in a vial full of clear liquid. She told them she felt fine and was just suffering from an allergy attack, but it didn't matter. They didn't believe her and drug her, kicking and screaming, from the gym.

On the ride to the jail, terror descended over her mind, crushing rational thought. She didn't know what would happen to her mom, Uncle Reed, or Turner. Even the constant fear when on the streets, so strung out she didn't care what she had to do to survive long enough to get more money for another hit, paled in comparison to what was happening now.

The soldiers dumped her in the last cell and left without saying a word. She had recognized two Hot Spring County deputies stationed at the front. She begged them to vouch for her, but they never said a word. When they escorted her down the hallway, she nearly fainted because the cells were full of men and women, some crying, others begging to be released. She recognized some of the faces but not all. Every one of them looked sick; several were coughing, others sitting on the floor, unmoving, gazes focused on the ground.

The walls are closing in around her—she despises being closed in. The building blocks out most of the sounds of the world ending outside, but the noises replacing it from the inside make her head spin. The crying and begging for help ceased ten minutes prior and now, the only thing she hears is weird, gurgles and grunts. The eerie noises push her to the precipice of a full meltdown. Heat blossoms from her chest up into her neck as her breath comes in short bursts.

A full-blown panic attack is on the verge of consuming her entire being, and for the first time in two years, Jesse wished she was high.

"Hey, honey, you okay over there?"

Jesse stops pacing and turns toward the front. Inside the cell across the aisle are three women, none who appear familiar, but she doesn't care. "No…having…a…panic…attack."

A lady close to her mom's age with a warm, inviting face, smiles. "My mom used to have them all the time. Said the trick to stopping one was to concentrate on a spot on the floor or ceiling."

The young girl next to her reaches into her bra and pulls out a baggie. "This has always worked for me. Keeps my head straight when things go to shit. And boy, did things ever go to shit."

Jesse's eyes wide while watching the girl tap out a line of white powder on the back of her other hand. She doesn't have time to figure out if it is coke or meth because the girl lowers her head and snorts it up.

"Eileen, what are you doing? Are you crazy? You brought drugs in here? Shit! What if someone sees you?"

"I don't think those goons out there give a fuck if I'm high, Aunt Carrie. They're too concerned with killing people, or haven't you noticed? If this is the end of the line for me, which I'm pretty sure it is for all of us, I'm going out on a high note. Literally."

"We aren't gonna die. We ain't sick, Eileen. They'll realize that soon enough and let us go. You watch and see."

"Grow up, Susie." Eileen licks the remaining traces of powder from her hand. "You don't really think they'll come back for us, do you?"

"Enough, you two." Carrie admonishes. "We need to stay positive. Besides, we're safe in here from all the mess going on outside."

Seeing her own personal demon less than ten feet away, plus watching another person get high, the temptation is too much for Jesse. Unable to really form words, she pats the bars.

Eileen looks over and smiles. "You want?"

She nods, and the girl closes the baggie and tosses it across the aisle into her cell. Without thinking, she opens the baggie and tries to tap some out, but her shaking fingers refuse to cooperate.

"No, honey, you don't need that to calm down!" Carrie's voice is loud yet somehow soothing. "Another thing that works is listening to someone's voice talk you down. Ain't nothing nice to look at in this hellhole so just focus on the sound of my voice. Put that poison down, okay?"

Mind in full gridlock and unable to speak, Jesse nods. The woman sings *Amazing Grace* and though off-key, Jesse does care. Closing her eyes, she sings along inside her mind, the words memorized from years of attending Sunday school.

For a few seconds, the craving to snort up what is in her hands abates.

As the kind woman nears the end of the first chorus, Eileen and Susie joined in.

"I once was lost, but now I'm found. Was blind, but now I see..."

Jesse's stops hyperventilating. Her breathing returns to normal at the soothing words of the song. She opens her eyes and notices the trio joined hands, their eyes closed as they sway back and forth.

The calmness inside her mind last only seconds as the baggie's contents calls out to her.

They aren't watching. Go ahead! I'll be better prepared to handle things when all my nerves are on heightened alert. Besides, I'll probably need the extra burst of energy to stay awake.

The demon in her hands wins the battle. Jesse opens the baggie and sticks her nose inside. Judging from the smell, she immediately knows it is cocaine and not meth, but right now, she doesn't care. Just as she readies herself to snort up the contents, a booming voice from the aisle rings out.

"Give it a rest, will you? Y'all sound like a bunch of howler monkeys."

She freaks as Sheriff Calhoun shuffles down the aisle. She's always hated the man, and not just because he'd arrested her once. With nowhere to hide the plastic bag, she shoves it into her mouth and swallows, nearly choking.

Calhoun is a stereotypical southern cop in every sense of the word. Loud, brash, cocky, and full of himself. His large belly stretches the material of his uniform to its limits; gut so big it hides the belt. He has a fat, round face, and the meanest eyes of anyone Jesse has ever met.

Today, he looks even worse. Sweat stains the front and sides of his shirt. Droplets of water glisten on his forehead under the fluorescent lights in the ceiling. His cheeks are flushed, and his eyes glaze over. Even though he is several feet away, Jesse can tell he has a fever.

Jesus, is he infected, or simply has a cold? How is anyone supposed to tell anymore? No wonder the soldiers brought me here. They didn't know for sure, either.

"Sheriff, we were just trying to help calm the poor girl down. She's scared to death."

Sheriff Calhoun stops in front of the cell housing the three women. "I don't give a shit. I said stop your caterwauling. My head is already pounding!"

"You ain't got no right to hold us in here, Sheriff! We done told y'all we all just got over the flu. We ain't infected. And you can't stop us from singing." Eileen glares at the man.

Sheriff Calhoun doesn't answer the girl's outburst. Instead, he turns and focuses his attention on Jesse.

His eyes are bloodshot, his face now the same ugly, gray color as the concrete floors. A thin dribble of saliva slides from his open mouth. The veins under his skin darken, almost like an invisible hand holding a blue marker draws them on. His mouth opens and closes like he is talking, but no sound accompanies the movement.

This isn't happening!

The women across from Jesse continue to berate the man, but their words seem muffled and distant.

The Sheriff's entire body jerks. Looking down, she notices a chunk of flesh is missing from his hand, and when she brings her gaze back to his face, notices his eyes are now solid black.

She moves away from the bars and doesn't stop until her back hits the wall.

Sheriff Calhoun spins around and lunges at the women in the cell. His sudden movements catch them off guard, and the nice lady with the sweet face named Carrie doesn't have time to move away from the bars. His arm shoots out and grabs a handful of her long, brown hair. Yanking her forward, her face slams into the bars. Blood spurts out of her lips and nose from the impact.

The man makes a weird grumbling sound before his head lurches forward, tearing off chunks of Carrie's protruding lips and nose from in between the bars. The women scream in terror.

Unable to help, trapped inside a cage as the next victim, Jesse cannot believe what she was witnessing.

For a few seconds her mind is totally gridlocked. She regains her faculties when the thing that had once been human only seconds before, tears the arm off at the elbow of the lady with the horrible singing voice and then shuffles down the hall, crouches down next to the door, and begins eating.

Jesse's stomach revolts and she pukes harder than she ever has in her entire life, even when detoxing. After vomiting, she screams at the top of her lungs for help, knowing it won't do any damned good.

Chapter 18 - Discovering the Truth

Saturday December 20th – 9:45 a.m.

EVERETT'S THIGH MUSCLES throb and his calves burn. He hasn't walked so far in years, and in the current conditions, the trek through the woods adds to the difficulty level. He is breathing hard, and the cold rain makes his bones ache.

"Do we need to stop and let you catch your breath?" Dirk looks at him, concern furrowing his brow.

"No. I'm fine. Maybe just slow down a bit? This incline is taking its toll on my legs."

Dirk snaps his fingers to get the attention of the six others walking in front of them. They all stop, and he points to a fallen tree to the right. "We've got time to rest, Dr. Berning. No one is out here except us."

He steps over to the downed tree and sits, hating the idea of remaining out in the open, yet his body is grateful for a moment to rest. "How much farther do we have?"

Dirk sits next to him and hands him a bottle of water. He twists off the cap and takes several gulps.

"About half-a-mile."

Everett looks over at the men who are about twenty feet away, silent, each fully armed and scanning the wet, quiet woods. One of them holds a walkie-talkie to his ear, and the look of worry on his face make his own fears increase.

These are hardened, former soldiers—ones who've witnessed deplorable conditions before— and even they are scared.

He chuckles softly and shakes his head.

"What?" Dirk asks.

"Oh, just glad I'm not the only one freaked out, that's all."

Dirk takes a swig of water and nods. "No, you aren't. I can't speak for all of them, but I know I've seen some disturbing shit over the years. Human beings are the most vicious creatures on the planet, and capable of vile and disgusting acts. I've seen my share of people wearing the mask of humanity that hid the monsters inside them. You know, fools willing to slaughter others for one stupid reason or another. Political, religious, oil rights, territory squabbles, money, race, creed, or even no reason at all. We are a violent breed. The only difference now is the ones slaughtered don't remain dead."

"No, it seems they don't." Giving such an answer makes him feel sick inside, like he's slipped off the platform of sanity and is freefalling into madness. Deciding the moment is as good as any, he decides to ask the question that's been bothering him for the last few hours. "Why are you doing this?"

"Doing what?"

"Wasting your precious time getting to safety to let an old man rest. Risking your lives to help me. I mean, I'm worthless to all of you now. I've spent the last year trying to recreate a formula it took me ten years to create and haven't had any success yet.

Even if I had, it's pointless now. I'm no longer useful."

"Now is not the time to have a pity party, Dr. Berning." Dirk raises an inquisitive eyebrow. "Just because the world never found out about your discovery doesn't mean a damned thing. We know you did, which makes you invaluable."

"How so? I don't think fighting drug addiction is still on the radar. There are more important things to fight for now."

"Exactly! And who better to help do so than the brilliant mind of the man who found a cure for drug addiction? Something no one ever thought possible except Drs. Thomas and Flint. Oh, and you."

"Are you crazy? Whatever in the hell is going on is way beyond my scope of knowledge. Besides, I don't have a sample to test, or the proper facilities to keep such a volatile pathogen. It took ten years for me to find the cure, and I doubt any of us have another ten years left."

"Excuses, Dr. Berning. A sample would be easy to obtain, and worrying about releasing a contagious disease on the population is sort of a pathetic joke now, don't you think? I'm not going to even acknowledge the crack about age."

"No, no way. Again, out of my scope and expertise. Finding out whatever is turning people into...things...is a job for those at the CDC. A group, a team, all sporting a collective IQ in the thousands."

"I call bullshit." Dirk leans closer and lowered his voice. "You did what no one else could, and with only two other researchers to assist you. I know the loss of your family is what drove you to not give up. You spent ten fucking years, every day without taking even one day off. In my book, that's determination. That's grit. And that's the kind of man we need working on solving this cluster fuck some lesser scientist got us in to. In other words, Dr. Berning, we are doing this because you matter. To us. To the world."

"Nice speech, Kincanon. Very powerful. Sounds eerily similar to the one Dr. Flint gave me many years ago."

Dirk laughs. "Probably because I wrote it out and made her memorize it."

Everett shakes his head. "Figures."

"So, pep talk over. You're a genius and possibly the new savior of mankind. Back to our discussion about the current situation and why it's happening. I know you said you didn't have much time to watch the reports before the EBS took over, but what you did see—did it give you any clues as to what we are dealing with? In all my years of training, I've never seen or heard of a biological, even a weaponized one, react this way on human flesh."

"None. I'm just as in the dark as everyone else. Venturing a guess would be just that—a guess."

"Do you think some twisted individual muted or combined strains of several things? Is it even possible to mix viruses like Ebola and Marbug together? Maybe someone created a super-strain?"

Everett waits to answer until the screaming jets overhead pass by. The heavy rainclouds block them from seeing the planes, but he doesn't care. Just hearing them is enough. It means there is still hope.

"That's one possible scenario. If a cell is introduced to multiple viruses at the same time, the viruses can recombine in one of two ways. Genomic strands can be crossed over, or a re-assortment of the genomic segments. The results would be a new virus, and the physical properties of the new strain would depend upon how the recombination occurred. That rarely happens, though. Most of the time, the host suffers from the effects of both diseases until the deadlier one wins out. Viruses attack a host cell, not each other."

"But it can, and does, happen, right?" Dirk presses.

"Yes. The term is called antigenic shift. When two or more different strains of a virus, or even separate viruses, combine, the new pathogen created retains the surface antigens of both the original strains. That's how the primate virus mutated and formed HIV."

"With all the insane fools in other countries willing to do anything to validate their twisted agendas, maybe some rogue scientist figured out how to combine rabies and Ebola? What I saw sure looked like rabid humans. Doesn't rabies destroy the brain and make the infected go mad?"

"Yes." Everett shivers at the thought. "Rabies causes encephalitis in brain tissue. However, the incubation period after exposure is at least four days or more."

"Unless someone figured out how to modify it."

"Sir! You need to hear this!"

Their conversation is interrupted by Kevin Warton's panicked voice. Dirk and Everett both stand and join the others. The men all have the same shocked expression on their faces.

"What is it Warton?"

Kevin holds the walkie-talkie to his mouth and pushes the button. "Repeat last transmission."

Over the crackle of static, a male voice responds, "All of Camelot is down. Karate in place. Everywhere. We're on our own."

"Who the hell was that?" Dirk asks.

"My brother-in-law, David. He's Secret Service. Or he was."

"What the hell did all that mean?" Everett whispers, though the burning inside his chest already knows the answer.

Dirk rubs his temples, the stress of the words apparent. "It means the White House and Pentagon no longer are functioning and all high-level government and military personnel are incapacitated or dead. We are now under martial law."

Everett leans against the tree closest to him for support, fearing he will faint. "This fast? I can't believe it! God, it can't get any worse, can it?"

Dirk's face hardens with determination. He points toward the trail. "We need to get moving and underground. Now. "

The others follow the instructions and trot ahead. Dirk glances over to Everett and frowns. "And yes, it can get worse. All of Camelot means the entire globe."

Overhead, another jet passes over, but this time, it is louder and much closer.

"Take cover! It's coming in hot!"

Dirk's body slams into his and then they both smash into the hard ground. Dirk's heavy torso covers his view of the sky, but not the sound of an engine closing in and in seconds, the noise is replaced by a deafening explosion. The wet ground rumbles underneath them.

Dirk rises and helps Everett to his feet. "Welcome to Hell, doc."

Dirk turns and jogs away, leaving Everett alone and frightened. He cannot think of anything to say in response. His mind is blank, so he simply follows in the steps of the others, oblivious now to the pain in his muscles and joints.

What have we done to ourselves? How long will we last? How long will society last? Will I have enough time to figure out how to stop this? What if I can't?

Minutes later, when the ragtag group reaches the entrance to the lab, he is so numbed by the events he doesn't even smile because the weight of the world on his shoulders won't let him.

Chapter 19 - Painful Choices

THOUGH DISGUSTED BY THE horrible sight in front of her, and the fact she is going to kill someone she's known for over thirty years, Regina doesn't hesitate. She fires three shots into the bald head of Sheriff Calhoun. He drops to the ground with a sickening thud, blood and brain matter oozing from his destroyed head.

"Dear God." Allsop closes his eyes. "This ain't happening."

"Shoot the head." Regina instructs. "Every last one of them. Right now. We can't afford for them to get out."

"But that's Malvern's quarterback Raymond Wright!"

"Not anymore, Bailey. Put him down."

The man hesitates, fingers and lips trembling. Turner exchanges glances with Regina before stepping past the shocked deputy, nudging him aside. "I got this, Bailey."

A single shot from Turner's weapon silences the monster wearing a Malvern Leopards t-shirt, running shorts and Nike's.

The same scene is played out ten other times as the group make their way down the long aisle. Once familiar faces—people she's seen at Walmart or the gas station or church or even pulled over—are now vile monsters. They stick their arms through the bars, clawing, hissing, and biting until a bullet ends their suffering.

The floor in front of the cells at the end of the hallway is covered with blood and gore. The screaming changes over to low whimpers.

Regina isn't sure if they are from the living or dead.

With Turner at her side, they walk the remainder of the distance until reaching the end of the row.

Three women are on the floor. Regina's knees almost gave out from relief upon realizing Jesse isn't among them. Glancing behind her, she catches a glimpse of her daughter in the other cell, relief washes over her soul. Turning back around, she notices blood covers the floor, walls, and their clothes. One girl is on the left side of a lady stretched out on the floor, holding a stiff pillow against what is left of an arm. The other woman's head rests in the lap of a young girl. The faintest whisper of *Amazing Grace* comes from the girl's mouth.

Knowing the woman will turn any second, she must get the girls out without sending them into a panic. They've already been through enough. Glancing at Turner, she can tell he knows exactly what she is about to do as he nods and steps forward, unlocking the cell door.

Regina clears her throat. "Come on, ladies. We're gonna get her some help now. Y'all have done a fine job. We'll take it from here."

"Like hell!" The younger one yells, continuing to stroke the blood-matted hair. "Look what he did to her—he ripped part of her face off, and y'all just killed everyone in here in seconds! Think I'm gonna trust you?"

The woman on the floor holding a pillow against her arm groans as her legs twitch. No more blood leaks from her mouth and nose as her eyes roll back in her head and she begins shaking.

Regina bursts inside, grabbing the arm of the young girl on the right. She yanks her from the floor and pushes her straight into Bailey's arms. The girl hurls a mouthful of cusswords she doesn't recognize. With the only girl who will survive safely out of the cell, she looks at Turner and mouths, "Hold her."

Bailey turns the girl in the opposite direction so she cannot see her friends die.

Thankful the woman's features on the floor are so distorted she doesn't look human Regina holds her breath and fires. One shot, dead center between the eyes. Taking aim, she fires off a second round, ending the life of the girl convulsing on the floor in the back of the cell.

Once finished, she rushes to Jesse's cell.

"Mom!" Jesse whimpers from the floor.

Curled into a ball in the corner of the room in pink pajamas, tears running down stained cheeks and eyes wild with fear, Jesse looks like a little girl. Fresh vomit covers the front of her pajamas and the floor. Grateful she is alive, knowing they arrived with only seconds to spare, she struggles to unlock the door fast enough so she can hug her only child.

"Baby," Regina gushes, wrapping her arms around Jesse's neck and squeezing tight. "You okay? Sheriff Calhoun didn't bite or scratch you, did he?"

"I'm okay, and he didn't hurt me, but oh, my God…he ripped her arm off, Mom! Ripped it off and then ate it. When I saw that, I threw up and started screaming. I thought this was it for me."

Jesse falls apart, sobbing uncontrollably. Regina knows she's in shock and must get her daughter out of there, but not before she calms down. To escape the jail, they will all need to be quiet.

Motioning for Turner to come inside, they grab Jesse's arms and lead her out of the cell and down the hallway.

"Shhh, baby." Turner coos softly. "It's okay. We're here."

"Yeah, and so are we."

They all turn to the sound of Walter Addison's voice. Lamar is right next to him and both men look shaken. Regina's stomach drops when she notices Walt is dressed in a fresh pair of fatigues.

"Where's Reed?"

"Out front with Martha. Got their hands full guarding a slew of grunts."

"Oh, Jesus! What happened in here?" Lamar looks past Regina toward the bloody cell block.

"Seriously, you can't figure that out?" She rolls her eyes. "Walt? I thought y'all were standing guard outside?"

"Yep, until two of them broke off to piss close to our hiding spot. Some heavy shit came across the radio. We've got several problems." Walt looks around and grimaces. "Dammit, I knew we shoulda left sooner!"

"Really, Dad?" Turner hugs Jesse close, like he is trying to shield her from the words.

Regina glowers at Walt, refusing to respond and add more fuel to the fire. They are all on edge for a variety of reasons and dressing him down now won't help calm the flames.

"Let's get out of here first. The smell's making me sick." Bailey looks down at the young girl who's clinging to him like a frightened toddler. He guides her as they step over the remains of the sheriff, hand clamped over her eyes, shielding her from the disgusting sight.

Jesse touches Regina's shoulder and squeezes. "Get me out of this hellhole, Mom. I don't ever want to see the inside of a jail again."

The entire group leaves the cell block in silence, none of them willing to look back at the carnage around them.

***

Once out in the main waiting area and able to breathe without gagging, Regina grimaces. Reed and Martha have lined up the soldiers against the wall inside the first lock station and they are all handcuffed.

"Turner? Trade spots with me. Chief's bleeding again." Martha nods toward her son.

"I'm fine." Regina's response seems to fall on deaf ears because the two switch places.

"Sit. We need you healthy." Martha turns her attention to the girl shaking in Bailey's arms. "What's your name, honey?"

"Susie." The young girl's voice is barely above a faint whisper.

Regina gives Susie the once-over, guessing she's close to fifteen. "How are you feeling okay? Any fever? Were you scratched or bit?"

"Yes, I'm okay. We all were getting over the flu and were on our way to Conway from Texas. We stopped at Walmart to get some medicine when the soldiers grabbed us."

"Was that your mom and sister?" Jesse asks.

"No. Aunt and sister. We went to live with her after our parents died last year. Aunt Carrie just got a new job, and we were on our way to our new place in Conway." Susie wipes away the tears streaming down her cheeks.

The pain in her words make Regina's heart melt for the poor girl. She is thankful the girl doesn't seem infected. "Any other family close-by?"

Eyes so green and full of pain they shimmer, Susie looks at her and shakes her head.

"Don't worry, Susie. We'll take care of you. Promise."

Martha clears her throat. "Why don't you and Jesse come over here and have a seat next to the Chief. Turner? Grab some paper towels from that bathroom. Get them wet and let's get these girls here cleaned up."

Turner disappears inside the bathroom, returning with a handful of damp towels. He offers some to Jesse and Susie. The young girl is too traumatized to reach out for any, so Regina nudges Jesse's arm.

"Here, let me help you." Jesse wipes the blood and gore off Susie's cheeks.

Regina turns her attention to the men on the other side of the bars. No, they aren't men. They are boys, and all but one appear barely old enough to buy alcohol. Their haughty attitudes from before are no longer visible. The looks on their faces are dead giveaways—they are scared.

Forcing herself not to wince as Martha patches her up, Regina looks at Walt. "What happened?"

Walt paces back and forth in front of the reception desk, clearly worried. "Ain't no way to say this easy, so I'll just spit it out. The White House and Pentagon have been overrun and ain't no longer running the show. The internet is down, and so are the land lines and cell towers. Power's still on, but at this rate, I don't know for how long."

Regina's mouth drops open, yet no words come out. She is too stunned to say anything. Instead, she reaches out her hand and finds Jesse's.

"Martial Law has been declared," Walt continues. "According to the conversation we heard between them boys and their lieutenant, all untested citizens are to be terminated immediately. They got a handle on the few infected that snuck inside the gym earlier, and now they're just staying put, barricaded inside, waiting for straggler troops to return. Once everyone is accounted for and they're finished with carrying out the order, the troops are to evacuate the area and return to base."

"Ain't no way! You must have heard wrong. They wouldn't do that—just leave us on our own to fight those things—try and survive without help? No. No way. I don't believe it. The government wouldn't kill innocent civilians either!" Allsop runs over to the bars. "Right? Tell them they misunderstood!"

"Are you for real? Surely you aren't so naïve?"

"No one asked you to open your trap," Walt yells at the soldier who answered. "Don't open it again because I'll be more than happy to shut it. Permanently."

"Enough!" Regina yells, gaze focused on the soldier while squinting to read his name tag. She is too far away to make out his name, so she counts Chevron's and tries to remember what rank two stripes signify. "Corporal, right?"

"Yes, ma'am. Corporal Gary Bennett."

"I'm Regina Parker, Chief of Police in Rockport. No time for games or to pussyfoot around. Be straight with me, and I promise the same. Is that the plan? To kill innocent people and then scurry out of town?"

Cpl. Bennett nods, unwilling to look her in the eye.

Anger boiling, she brushes Martha's hand away and stands. "Would Lt. Pack be the one who gave the go-ahead to slaughter the residents of my county?"

"That'd be the one." Cpl. Bennett answers.

Regina turns her gaze toward Reed and Walt, afraid if she looks at the corporal any longer, she'll snap. "Where is this upstanding man?"

"He's at the school. All personnel are to report there to help. They want to leave the county by noon."

She looks over at her daughter then to Reed—her reasons for living. Hundreds of other people crammed inside the high school feel the same for their loved ones, which means there is simply no way she can just leave. If she abandons them now, so much blood will be on her hands she'll drown in a sea of guilt.

She won't leave, even if the decision means the red clay of Hot Spring County will be her final resting place. With the first dilemma cleared, she focuses on exactly what their next moves should be.

Walking over to the bars, she peers at all the men. "I'm not gonna let my town, my county, go without a fight. It's as simple as this: you're with us or against us. Raise your hand if you are still loyal to our traitorous government."

All but two, including Cpl. Bennett, raise their hands. Disgusted by the misguided priorities, she gives them a curt nod and walks away over to the rest of the group, motioning for them to move to the front door and out of earshot of the others.

She waits to speak until they are far enough away the others cannot hear. "Walt? You're the tactical one and have the most experience dealing with the military and their procedures. Any ideas?"

"Yeah, get the hell outta dodge."

"We ain't gonna leave the residents of our town to be slaughtered like sheep!" Martha interjects.

"Two hours ago, we were." Walt counters.

"Things have changed dramatically since then." Martha huffs. "We're staying."

"I know, I know." Walt sighs. "I'm just blowing steam here. Okay, so we've got about an hour to do this. We can each take a Humvee and head to the school, grab as many people as our said vehicle can hold, get them to safety, and continue the extraction until ain't none left."

"What if the soldiers at the school start asking questions, or try to stop us?" Reed asks.

"We'll just tell them the orders changed, and we are to take them to the morgue to be incinerated. I guarantee you right now, those soldiers inside are just as scared and freaked as we are, so the less people they must worry about on their plate, the better."

"So where are we really taking them?" Turner asks, clearly confused. "We can't take them all home. Too time consuming and risky. Are we bringing them back here, or maybe the hospital?"

"Actually, I have a better idea." A shit-eating grins spreads across Walt's lips. "The place is big, insulated, has food, water, medicine, clothing, bathrooms, and much more. It's a perfect spot to keep everyone."

Regina returns Walt's smile. "Walmart. Yes, perfect!"

Walter nods. "Every southerner's second home, right?"

Regina looks over to Reed, who's staring out the front window. "What do you think, brother?"

"I think that's the best plan I've heard all day. I'm afraid we aren't going to have time to change clothes, though. Company's coming."

The rest of them turn and look out the window. A large group of infected, maybe one hundred or more, are in the parking lot across the street. They aren't moving yet their attention seems focused on the jail.

Regina's stomach churns. "Jesse—you and Susie come with me. We'll get to Walmart, secure the front glass doors, and lock the back bay doors until we hear one of you drive up."

"You'll need help moving stuff," Turner adds. "I'll come too."

"We'll need all the help driving we can get, son." Martha shakes her head. "You need to come with us. Chief Parker can handle things on her own."

"Mom, I need…"

"It's okay, babe." Jesse interrupts. "We got this,"

"Fine. We got our instructions. Time to quit yapping and move!" Reed points toward the street. "They're coming."

"Keys are all in the ignitions. Scatter!" Walt yells.

"What about us? You can't just leave us here!" Cpl. Bennett yells.

"Don't worry. The bars will keep you safe." Regina's features harden. "If we survive, we'll be back. That's a promise. Unlike your folks, I took my oath to serve and protect to heart."

Bailey opens the glass doors and the group scatters, each running to a Humvee. The sounds of screaming men from inside fade away as Regina, Jesse, and Susie jump inside a vehicle and close the doors.

"This is never going to work, Mom! Never!"

Regina cranks up the Humvee, guns the engine. Grips the steering wheel and holds on tight while dodging the dead descending on the parking lot. "Before today, the dead rising and walking around was never a consideration either. The word 'never' doesn't hold the weight it used to any longer. Put your seatbelts on. This will be the craziest trip to the store. Ever."

Jesse shakes her head while muttering, "Guess I won't be late for my shift after all."

ABOUT THE AUTHOR

Award-winning and International bestselling author, Ashley Fontainne, is an avid reader, becoming a fan of the written word in her youth, starting with the Nancy Drew mystery series. Stories that immerse the reader deep into the human psyche and the monsters lurking within us are her favorite reads.

www.ingramcontent.com/pod-product-compliance
Lightning Source LLC
Chambersburg PA
CBHW031322170626
46807CB00002B/530